Going Forward

Going Forward

Richard Schalhamer

Windysun Publishing
Golden, Colorado
Windysunpublishing.com

ISBN: 978-0-578-32772-3

CONTENTS

CHAPTER 1
The Diner

"Hey, if anyone is alive back there, I need to stop and at least get a cup of coffee so I can halfway stay awake," Rick yelled from the driver seat.

No one answered, which meant that everyone was either sound asleep or dead. He was on his own, which he knew was the case for the last four hours of driving.

Rick and three other army buddies had been on an extended leave trip to Key West, where they had spent the last five days scuba diving and partying more than their bodies should allow. It was a great trip and a well-deserved break from the military life they had been leading for the last six months. The sun and surf, however, had just taken everything out of all of them. So, everyone was dead-to-the-world, sleeping in the back of Ed's 1968 blue Chevy van, including Ed. It was not that late, 2100 hours, but it was dark, and the highway was vacant, as it was a Sunday night. Up ahead and off to the right were the dim lights of a flashing diner sign, so Rick decided to pull in for just a quick cup of coffee and a bathroom stop. The parking lot was empty, and everything looked to be closed, but the sign on the door was still flipped to the open side. Rick decided to park the van and go inside.

"I'm going in for a cup of coffee and a pee. Does anybody want to join me?"

The silence from the back of the van was a good hint that no one was stirring, so he shut off the engine and headed for the diner's door. As he opened the glass door to what looked like an oversized mobile home, he could see that he was the only one in the place. It was a small place with only maybe ten tables and a long counter with bright, red-topped stools along the front.

"Can I help you?" a rough voice came echoing from a small window behind the long counter. "We are about ready to close up here, so don't be too fancy with what you want."

"I just need a strong cup of coffee," Rick replied with a reluctant tone.

"That's an easy one, young man, just have a seat at the counter there, and we will get you fixed up."

"Thank you, sir," Rick replied

"Mary, can you pour this young man a cup of coffee? I'm still in the middle of cleaning this goddamn grill."

"No problem, Uncle Bob, I'll get it," A soft voice answered, also amplifying out from the small window in the back of the counter.

Off to the far right of the long counter, two half swinging doors with wooden slats swung open, and out came a blur of pink. Rick assumed it was the waitress who belonged to the soft voice that came from the window. She gently put a five-pound bag of sugar that she was carrying on the far end of the counter. She then started walking along the back of the long counter towards Rick. He had sat down on one of the red stools at the counter. One of his elbows was on the counter with his chin resting in the palm of his hand. As she approached, the blur of pink became a striped waitress uniform. It was an older uniform that Rick had not seen in years. The ones with short sleeves, little starched white cuffs at the ends, and a matching white starched collar. Rick started to chuckle to himself at this old-style waitress garb, but then his eyes shifted to the beauty that was wearing it. His thoughts cleared for an instant as he felt his obsession with her grow as she neared. Her tan skin amplified the bright pink of her uniform, making it stand out

2

that much more in the dim lights of the diner. Her long flowing hair draped down over the starched white collar, almost hiding it from his view. Her hair was a shiny brown with scattered blonde hints, he assumed from being in the sun. Her hair partially hid her face and framed it nicely. When her brown eyes looked out from behind the hair drapes, all pink was forgotten and washed away. Only her natural beauty was in front of him.

"Hi, I'm Mary."

Before she could finish her sentence, Rick interrupted, "I know. I heard your name being called by the guy in the back."

"That's my Uncle Bob. He owns this place."

After a quick moment of them looking over each other, Mary continued her primary waitress duty.

"So, you need a little coffee, do you?"

"Yea, yes, I do," Rick stuttered back, still a little overwhelmed and shocked from the surprise encounter.

"Would you like cream with that?"

"Yes, please."

"Now, I have to warn you that we have not brewed a fresh pot of coffee since lunch, so this might have a little *zip* to it," The waitress said with an apologetic tone. "A *zip* like mud, if you know what I," Just as she was about to finish her apology, she looked up for the first time, and her eyes met Rick's blue eyes in mid-sentence, "mean."

After a long pause and a seemingly more extended silence, she said, "How about I brew a new pot for you as long as you will promise to drink at least two cups."

"I promise."

Rick sat with his right elbow still resting on the counter and his hand holding up his chin. His head was pointing down at the glassed-in pie display in front of him, but his eyes were rolled up, watching every move this pink lady made. He was trying not to be obvious, so he made wild eye trips back and forth between the two. She moved like a well-choreographed dance; every move

3

seemed like it had been rehearsed. The pie case was losing the glance race as Mary reached upward to get a package of coffee filters. Her pink skirt reached up with her, exposing undergarment lace and well-shaped, tanned calf muscles. She then moved with a smooth motion down to the floor, bending both knees so she could reach a coffee cup on a bottom shelf. This, of course, pulled her loosely fitting skirt tightly across her backside, revealing precise details of her slender figure. Rick found himself lifting himself a small amount off his seat to get a better angle. He had to do a quick emergency shift back to the pie case as Mary rose and turned with another smooth motion and set the coffee cup in front of him.

"Coffee will be ready in just a second. What was your name again?"

"Rick," Rick answered with almost an out-of-breath tone from all his intense observing.

"Well, Rick, since you have been staring at our homemade pies so intensely, I assume that you would like a piece with your coffee. The key lime pie was just made this afternoon."

Rick quickly thought *that if she knew I was looking at the pies, she knew I was looking at her. Nice move, Ricky boy.*

"A, that would be great. They do look nice."

Rick found himself stumbling with words, which usually did not happen with him, especially around women. He had always been easygoing and carried the reputation among his friends that he could flirt with the best of them. Something was going on here which was blocking all his best lines and moves. He thought that maybe it was because he was so tired from all the driving.

"Here you go, sir, one key lime pie."

"Thanks."

"And some freshly brewed coffee," Mary said as she poured coffee into Rick's cup.

Rick quickly downed a few gulps of the black wake-up juice. With a big smile and a cheerful tone, she added." If you need anything else, just yell. You do not have to yell. This place is not that big. You could whisper, and I could hear you from the back wall." She laughed out loud, "I am sort of babbling on here, aren't I? Sorry, that is not like me. It has been a long day."

Rick was a little relieved to hear Mary babbling on as it made him forget his awkwardness and his own word stumbling.

"I have to agree with you on that one. I have been driving for four hours."

After a seemingly long pause, Mary bubbled out," Can I get you anything else?"

"How about some company?"

Now that is more like it, Rick thought as he said it. *That is the Rick that we all know and love.*

Mary, looking around the diner and then back towards the little window where her uncle was working. "It is not on the menu, but we are a little slow right now, so, sure, we can do company."

After pouring Rick some more coffee, Mary took off her small apron and walked around the counter and sat on the stool next to him. She flipped her long hair back behind her ear with her right hand, and with her elbow on the counter, she rested the side of her head in her hand. She turned just her head to face Rick. Mary did have the most beautiful brown eyes that complimented her brown hair so well. Her eyebrows were naturally thin. Her smile lit up her whole face and made her upper cheeks flare out slightly, framing and amplifying her smile.

"So, what are you doing in these parts, stranger?"

"Three of my friends and I are coming back from a diving trip in the Keys. I was driving, and they were all sleeping in the back of the van. The road was starting to move on me, so I figured I needed to stop in here for a cup of your coffee and, of course, this world-famous key lime pie."

Rick took a big bite of pie.

5

"Where are you heading?"

"Augusta."

"Georgia?"

"That's the place."

"You do have a long way to go. Are you going to drive straight through?"

"Unfortunately, we have no choice. We have to line up for formation at 0600-hours."

"So, we are military, are we?"

"Yes, we are military, Army, if you must know," Rick said with a tone that expressed how much he hated it. "You are looking at one of the last of the draftees."

"Don't worry, you are not telling me anything that I did not already know. I sort of figured that you were military when you walked in the door."

"Yeah, right."

"There is a lot of militaries that pass through here, and you can usually spot them right away. Plus, that shorter hair that you have does stand out. This is the Seventies, you know, and it should be a little longer to be in style."

"Short hair, I'll have you know that I have the longest hair in my company, and it is a lot of work keeping it that way."

"A lot of work, what do you mean?"

"I really grease it down in the morning and do a lot of stuffing under my hat, so the higher-ups don't see me and make me cut it."

"Well, I'm glad you didn't grease it today. It looks very nice and long."

Mary reached over and gently brushed a few strands of Rick's hair out from in front of his eyes.

Realizing that she had just brushed her fingers through a stranger's hair, she pulled her hand back right away and acted as naturally as she could.

"You have some blonde hair. I bet that grease you put on it darkens it a few shades."

"Yes, it does," Rick answered, still in a bit of shock from the waitress's last move. He was a little uncomfortable, but at the same time, was getting sort of excited about this lady.

"How did your hair become so blonde?"

"Oh, I was born with it, and it never changed, I guess. Being in the sun and water so much does bleach it out a little."

"It sure does," Mary answered, staring at his hair.

Rick became a little uncomfortable again as he saw a look on Mary's face like she wanted to run her hands through his hair again. Usually, that would not bother him, but with this lady, it did. He was a little relieved yet disappointed when she didn't.

"Ok, you have a brief history of what I am doing in these parts. What are you doing here?"

"That is an easy one. I live here."

"Come on, you can do better than that."

"All right, I have lived here all my life."

"I don't mean to interrupt, but where am I, exactly?'

"Do you mean like this town, Lake City, or the state of Florida? Where did you think you were?"

"Sorry, but I sort of lost track of where I was driving when I fell asleep back in Gainesville."

Mary laughed and then looked slightly serious for a second, "You are joking, aren't you?"

"Of course, I am. I was quite a few miles north of Gainesville before I fell asleep."

"Come on, be serious," Mary said as she laughed and hit Rick on his upper arm.

"Ok, you have lived here, in Lake City, your whole life. What else?"

Mary still had her head resting in her hands when she looked up at the ceiling as if the answer was written there. "Well, after graduating from high school, I started working here at my uncle's diner to earn money for my college. I just got my Associate in Science Degree at Lake City Community College. With an emphasis on nursing. I always wanted to be a nurse. At the end of the summer, I am heading to Chicago to get my bachelor's degree."

"Chicago. Why Chicago?" Rick said.

"I have an aunt that lives there, and she is going to let me stay with her until I can find a place, and I am using her address, so I can get instate tuition."

"That's great," Rick said with a sincere look on his face. "All of that is tough to do. You should be pretty proud of yourself."

"Yea, I do believe I am."

"I remember working my way through college, and the pressure from all of my friends to blow my savings on a new car or a night on the town was always tremendous," said Rick

"Yes, I know what you mean. In fact, did your friends look at you like you were sort of weird? I know mine did."

Answering quickly, Rick replied," Many of them did. In fact, I lost some friends because of it. I was taking classes at the junior college and working at the same time, so I just didn't have the time to go out and party a lot like they did."

Mary finally lifted her head out of her hand and spun on the stool to look directly at Rick and said with excitement. "Yes, I know exactly what you mean. I have been taking three classes a semester at our junior college. With work and studies, there is not much time for anything else."

"Not even a boyfriend?" Rick was attempting to be sly and find out that critical bit of information without directly asking.

"No, not at the moment anyway."

With a noticeable relief in his voice, Rick answered back." Come on, I would think the local boys around here would be breaking down the front door of this diner. I mean, that pink uniform of yours is pretty hard to resist."

That comment got Rick another hit on the arm.

"Ouch! That one hurt a little more than the last one. Do you always beat on your paying customers so much?"

"Only the ones who deserve it," Mary answered back, laughing.

"Sorry, I probably did. The uniform is really kind of sexy, you know."

"Right."

"No, I mean it, it is."

"Well, thank you, I guess."

Rick was serious. With Mary's wild smile, her brown eyes framed by her flowing brown hair, the uniform was like the frosting on a delightful cake. Rick had always made jokes or wisecracks when his true feelings were about to be exposed. It had been his self-prescribed defense mechanism to keep relationships at a distance.

"I really didn't hurt your arm, did I?" Mary asked as she gently touched Rick's arm.

"No, of course not; it gave me a reminder that I missed my drill sergeants touch. Just kidding, you were very gentle and made your point very clear."

Rick reached up and touched Mary's hand that was still on his arm. Their eyes met again. This time the eye contact was

different. They looked deep into each other's eyes for the first time, seeing that something was connecting between them, more than the casual flirting.

"More coffee?" Mary asked as she pulled her hand away with a quick, smooth motion towards the coffee pot.

After a pause, Rick answered back. "No thanks, one more cup, and my bladder will not make it to Macon." After a pause, Rick continued, "That was crude, wasn't it? Sorry."

"Come on, I work in a diner. You should hear some of the trucker talks that I get in here. You are a saint."

"You know I was not making fun of your uniform. I really meant it when I said it was sexy."

"You are sweet, and I knew you meant it the first time you said it."

Just as Rick stretched out his hand to touch Mary's arm resting on the counter, the diner door opened with a crash.

"Hey, where is our driver?" Tom yelled out with a humorous but forceful tone.

He was followed by two other scruffy-looking companions who looked like they had just crawled out from a long night's sleep, which they had.

"What have you done with our Rick?" Ed yelled as he and his group walked towards Rick and Mary.

For some reason, Rick jerked back his hand from its rest position on Mary's arm and said," I am right over here, you morons."

"That has been one long cup of coffee, soldier," said Ed. I see you have been doing more than drinking coffee," as he gave a smirk and a glance at Mary. A rush flowed over both of their faces.

"You know we have another 5 hours of driving ahead of us and that 0600-hour roll call will not wait."

"I hear you, dad," said Rick.

"Ed, Ted, Tom, this is Mary," said Rick. "Mary, this is Ed, Ted, and Tom. Now you guys take care of your business, back there around the corner, and I will meet you in the van in a few minutes.

"Yes, drill sergeant," said Tom, as they all headed for the bathroom.

"That did sound like an order, didn't it?" Rick said as he turned his stool back to face Mary. "Sorry about that."

"No problem, boys will be boys."

"We do need to get going. Those guys are right. It is a long drive back to Augusta.

Rick hesitated then said," It was so lovely meeting you, and thanks for the coffee and the friendly conversation and laughs. It made my day for sure."

"You are so welcome, young man. It made my day also."

Mary reached out and placed her hand on top of Rick's, still on the counter where he had jerked it away earlier. Her hand felt warm and soft. This time he did not pull his hand away but put his other hand on top of hers.

With hesitation and a slight stutter, Rick blurted out, "What would you say if a certain guy that you just met would drop by a certain diner next Friday. And maybe take you out for a movie or something?"

Still, with her hand between Rick's, Mary said, "I would say to that certain guy that something like that sounds very nice."

Removing her hand from in-between Rick's, she got up from the stool and walked around the other side of the counter. Stopping in front of Rick, she pulled a pen out of her pocket and wrote something on her menu pad.

"Here is the number for the diner. I will be working here all day so it might be best to not call me at home. Why don't you give me a call next Friday when you get into town"?

She handed the note to Rick with a huge smile.

At that moment, the guys came out from the back bathroom. "Are you ready, Rickey boy," said Ed.

"Yes, I am, Edward! I will meet you guys in the van in just a moment."

"Would you boys like some coffee for the road," said Mary, "We will have to toss it out anyway."

"That would be great." said Ed, "Especially since my driving shift is next."

"None for me," Rick said. "I will be sleeping the rest of the trip."

"Tell those boys out there that we are closing now, and they need to get out of here." Came the voice from the window.

11

"Yes, Uncle Bob. We are closing now," Mary repeated using the window's exact words. Mary poured three cups of coffee in paper coffee cups and handed one to each of the guys as they passed the counter.

"Gotta go," Rick said as he turned and headed for the door. Turning back, he said, "Again, it was so nice meeting you."

"Ditto," said Mary, waving with her hand. "I look forward to seeing you next Friday."

"Ditto, back at you."

Ed was already in the driver's seat as Rick crawled into the side door.

"I thought I had better drive as you are probably dead tired from all of that *hustling* you were doing in that diner."

"Very funny."

"She is a sweet-looking lady," said Tom. "I sure noticed those brown eyes right away. Too bad we must play soldier at 0600-hours. You could have stayed longer and at least got her number."

Rick held up the piece of menu pad paper with a grin on his face and waved it back and forth a few times in the open air.

Looking in the rearview mirror, Ed said, "You are so our hero."

"Man, I knew it," said Ted. "So, when are you going to call her?"

"We are going out next Friday."

"You are, our hero," said Ted

"Aw, you guys," said Rick with a bashful tone. "Ok, let's hit the road. I am going to try and get some sleep."

As Ed started the engine, he said, "We are going to cut that 0600 roll call a little close this time."

As Rick lowered his head down on his duffle bag, he added, "And I just remembered I have to lead PT in front of the company tomorrow morning, shit."

"Well, you are our physical-training guy, you know," said Ted.

"The price you pay for that extra stripe on your arm," said Ed.

They took off for Augusta, and Rick was asleep before they hit the main highway. It is not necessary to wonder who he was thinking about as he fell asleep.

CHAPTER 2
On Post

It was 0300-hours before Rick, Ed, Ted, and Tom made it back to Augusta. By the time they unloaded all the dive equipment, stored it at Ed's house, and got back on post, it was 0400-hours. Ed lived in married-housing with his wife, Monika. It was almost like being a civilian while in the Army. It was a great place to store everyone's equipment, as that would never happen in the barracks on base. By the time Rick got back to his room, it was almost 0430-hours, an hour, and a half before roll call. Rick had his own space in the barracks, as he was the platoon sergeant of the company. At 25, Rick felt it was well worth the added responsibility with his extra stripe to not sleep in the mass bedroom with all the younger troops. Rick knew that there was no time to catch any more sleep. He just got dressed into his work fatigues and read. He was reading *The Sun Also Rises* by Hemingway, which he had read many times and never tired of.

The routine of Army life was predictable when in the states, especially when you were a short-timer. It was always a given that roll call was at 0600-hours sharp. This was followed by a PT session that Rick, as platoon sergeant, usually would lead. He did not mind, as it kept him in shape and got his blood flowing for the day, which he was sure the higher-ups had in mind. The nice thing about PT was that all you had to wear was Army fatigues and a T-shirt to roll call. The PT was not all that bad. Rick's platoon was all new recruits, usually fresh out of basic training, so they did pretty much anything he said. The workout was not that strenuous. Jumping jacks, sit-ups, a few upper arm twirls, squat thrusts, and of course, push-ups. It was then followed by a mile run around the parade field. After the mile run, the troops returned to the barracks and dressed for the day's duties. The recruits were all in the Signal School, so they would all go to their appropriate classrooms. Rick would teach an occasional class whenever he was called on to do so. If not teaching, the higher-ups would find him some duty to do, from overseeing a work detail to driving the post commander around.

Rick was called a short-timer, which meant that he had less than 6 weeks left before being discharged from the Army. That was not enough time for him to have regular duty at anything, so he was given whatever job needed to be done. Usually, they were jobs no one else wanted. Rick did not mind, as he liked the variety, and with less than six weeks left, he really did not care what he did. Today there was nothing on the roster, so he had to report to the company commander. Captain Marandi was also a short-timer, so he was easy to get along with. The two of them had been comrades from the beginning, serving together many times throughout their tour, including Vietnam. They were drinking buddies and partied a lot together. They had to keep their friendship a secret as officers were not allowed to fraternize with enlisted personnel.

"Good morning, Bud," Rick said as he walked through the companies office door. Bud was the company clerk, and the two of them were also good party and drinking buddies.

"Here to find out what fun things you get to do today, are you?" said Bud.

"Yes, always an exciting thrill. Door number 1, 2, or 3. Hope I win the car today."

Bud chuckled, "Just head on in. The captain is not doing much. The typical day for officers, you know." Bud said with an almost whisper tone.

"Good morning, sir," Rick said as he saluted and stood at attention in front of Captain Andy Marandi. "At ease, soldier," said the captain, "you can shut the door behind you, sergeant."

When the door shut, Captain Andy got up from his desk and stood in front of Rick.

" How was your diving trip?"

"It was pretty great down there, as usual. You need to come with us one of these times. You would love it."

"I just might take you up on that before I get out of here."

"How were things around here this weekend?"

"Same old shit," said Captain Andy. "I had to pull officer-of-the-Guard duty Friday night, so that was pretty exciting. You know how that leaves little time for anything else the rest of the weekend. You know how catching up on sleep works after that all night guard duty. I suppose you want to know what is in store for you today."

"Yeh, excuse me, yes sir," said Rick.

"Well, the Full-Bird [a colonel who is almost a general] needs a driver all day, so you need to go back to the barracks and take out that dress uniform and get spit and polished. Sorry, buddy."

"Crap," said Rick. "That means I have to be nice all day, opening doors, waiting around, not to mention all that God damn saluting. While I am here, Capitan. I would sure like to get to leave early next Friday. I happen to meet this lovely lady down in Lake City, and I have this date with her on Friday night."

"You asshole," said Andy. "How do you do it? You are always meeting these ladies somewhere?"

"Just lucky, I guess."

"You know it is pretty hard getting out of here early these days as we are pretty short-handed with all you draftees getting discharged."

"I know," said Rick.

"Tell you what, we have been asked to supply a Sergeant-of-the-Guard for the stockade on Wednesday. You know that you get the next day off if you do that. I could make your day off on Friday."

"That sounds like an excellent plan, Andy. I owe you one. Although stockade duty sucks so bad."

"Tell me about it. That was me last Friday. At least I can just walk around and not have to sit in that guard tower all night like you are going to have to."

"Shit, I know. The things we have to do for women, right."

Rick left to drive the Colonel wherever he needed to go.

Wednesday at 1500-hours, Rick reported to the guard officer at the stockade. He was issued the usual sidearm 45 semi-automatic and a 12-gauge shotgun. Rick had done this duty enough before that he knew the routine very well.

He climbed the tall ladder that went straight up into the guard tower. Opened a trap door and squeezed through the tiny opening into the tower room. Once in the guard tower, it was protocol to lock the trap door behind him so that no one could get in. This was his home for the next 15 hours. Meals were brought up, and he would get an occasional latrine relief. No books, radios, or anything that would distract him, was allowed in the guard tower. Rick never paid attention to this order and always snuck in a book. A flashlight was issued, but he always packed extra batteries. Today was no different, as he managed to tuck Ernest Hemingway into his pants to get past inspection.

He was required to hang out on the guard tower balcony with a shotgun in hand during the daylight hours. After hours he could sit in the guard tower and just stare out over the vacant yard. The yard was a big sandlot surrounded by a high fence with cantina wire wound in rolls around the top. The prisoners in the stockade were usually in the sand field courtyard, just milling around in small groups during the day. These were usually soldiers waiting for a dishonorable discharge or shipment to a civilian jail for trial. Their offences were either military or civilian. Either way, they usually were not very nice people. They always gave the guards or anyone around them a tough time. Today seemed quiet, which made Rick happy, as he was not in the mood for any out-of-the-ordinary incidences.

Rick just stood on the guard balcony holding his shotgun, watching over the yard.

"Hey, you asshole up there in your little house," One of the prisoners in the yard yelled up at him.

Rick just ignored the comment and stayed looking out over the yard.

"Hey, big mister sergeant boy, how much cock did you have to suck to get those stripes."

Rick still just looked straight ahead out over the yard.

More prisoners started gathering below his tower. More of them started shouting at him.

"You fuck head going to shoot us with that little pea shooter."

"You mother fucker couldn't hit anything if you tried."

"We are going to sleep tonight, are you.? You get to stay up all night."

This went on and on as more prisoners gathering right below Rick's tower. Rick tried to ignore them, but it was getting more difficult as they were shouting insults. There were probably 15 of them now at the gathering, and they all had something to say that was not in the *nice* categorie.

"We know that you cannot shoot us, you mother fucking lifer."

Rick finally thought *I do not have to put up with this crap from these guys. I have less than six weeks left in this Army, and I have done my time. These are pieces of shit criminals.*

As one last fuck-you came from the group, Rick looked around at the yard and found an open area in the sand. Without saying a word, he locked and loaded a 12-gauge shotgun round in the chamber. The pumping sound of the loading was enough to cause a hush over the crowd. He then carefully aimed at the open area in the yard next to the masses and pulled the trigger. The loud blast from the barrel and the resulting sand flying into the group sent the prisoners running frantically back into the stockade building. Where they stayed the rest of Rick's guard duty shift. When the other tower guard realized what was going on, he just waved at Rick and gave a sloppy salute, followed by a thumbs-up. Rick felt good and sat down and read Hemingway.

Rick unlocked his guard tower trap door and climbed down the long ladder at 0530 hours. He reported to the guard officer, turned in his weapons, and checked in at the 0600-hour roll call. Rick was pleased that he did not have to lead PT this morning, so he reported to the company commander.

"Morning Bud," Rick said as he walked by the clerk's desk on his way into the CO's office.

"Tough night?" Bud said.

"Stockade guard is always tough."

"You might be prepared, Rick, as there was a memo from the top about some rumors from the prisoners about a weapon's discharge last night."

"Thanks, Bud, for the heads up. I am sure it was just some rumors."

Rick opened the door to the commanding officer's office and stood at attention in front of Captain Marandi's desk.

"At-ease soldier," said the captain. "You can shut that door behind you. How are you doing, Rick? Tough night on guard duty?"

"Like I just told Corporal Bud, Stockade guard is always tough."

"Anything out of the ordinary."

"Naw, just the same old boring shit," said Rick.

"Excellent," said Captain Andy. "We need to keep those pieces of shit prisoners happy, don't we?"

"Yes, we do," said Rick. "In fact, they were so happy last night that they all went inside the stockade building before they were supposed to."

"Probably to get some reading in, I assume. You have a light day today as you are supposed to get some rest. Why don't you do a few barrack inspections and go get some shut-eye."

"Thank you, sir, I will."

"And see you at 0600-hours Monday morning, Sergeant." Captain Andy said with a slight wink.

"Yes, sir. Thanks, I owe you one, buddy," Rick said as he snapped to attention and saluted.

As he turned for the door, the captain added, "Let me know if she has a friend."

"That I will do, my friend."

CHAPTER 3
First Date

It had been a long week for Rick. His attitude for playing a soldier had been deteriorating quickly as his discharge date approached. He was pretty much just going through day-to-day motions of performing mediocre jobs around the post. Word of his short-timer status spread quickly around the post, which meant that he was left alone, and his actions were not of much concern. What kept him moving forward were his constant thoughts of Mary. Her long brown hair dancing on her shoulders and her pink waitress uniform got him through the morning physical training. Those sexy brown eyes and bright smile got him through guard duty. The thought of seeing her on the weekend got him through the week.

He was genuinely puzzled as to why this lady was bothering him so. Rick had learned to be very cautious with relationships. In fact, he had become pretty much a cynic on long-term partnerships with women. Many women and relationships had crossed his path, but a couple of heartbreaks before he was drafted turned him into an anti-relationship crusader. He was now convinced that love was lovely for a while, but it was best to bail out at the top of the game before things got sour. He was genuinely convinced that relationships would eventually die. So, his history had been to have a good time, and when things stopped going forward and stagnated, to move on before they went backward. Rick's philosophy had been put on hold for the time being. This Mary lady had been filling up all his thoughts.

When Friday came around, his Jeep had been packed and ready to go since the night before. The final duty call was let out early on Friday, so Rick could leave Augusta by 1000-hours. It was about a five-hour drive to Lake City, so he arrived in the late afternoon. It took Rick a little while to find Mary's diner, as the last time he was in Lake City it was covered in darkness. Not to mention being half asleep. When he got on the right street, finding the diner was easy, as its flashing neon sign was like a beacon calling to him. He drove past it and found a Holiday Inn just a mile up the road. When he had talked with Mary earlier in the week, she had said she could get off work around six o'clock. That was fortunate, as it gave him time to rest from his long drive. Leaving Fort Gordon so quickly, he did not have time to shower or even change out of his uniform, so the extra time was welcomed. The time was also nice, as it gave him some time to relax and mentally get ready for the evening. He found that he would need the extra time as some excess anxiety had traveled along with him. Stress that he usually did not have.

Rick walked into the diner with a revitalized confidence that he had worked on very hard during the drive from the Holiday Inn. He sat at the counter, which looked different in the daylight, but still had a familiar sit. Concentrating on the swinging doors where he figured Mary would be coming out, he did not see her approach him from the other side of the diner.

"Hey there handsome, can I get you anything?"

Rick turned quickly with a jerking spin on his swivel stool, tipping over a saltshaker, and almost knocked the coffee pot out of Mary's hand with his shoulder.

"Settle down soldier, that stool will buck you right off. I didn't startle you, did I?"

"Oh no, I just wanted to see how far that coffee pot would fly if I knocked it out of your hand."

"Sorry," Mary said in a low apologetic voice. "Here, let me put this flying coffee pot down, and I will be right back."

Mary walked down and around the far end of the counter. Rick found himself fluttering along with the flow of her pink uniform as he watched. This lady who had been on his mind all week, was now real, and right in front of him. The darkness of the diner last week had not allowed him the view what he was now getting a complete picture of. Mary's tight uniform was now being taxed to its limits with her movement below her waist. As one of his old army buddies from the hills of North Carolina would say, *it looks like two Possums trying to get out of a gunnysack. Two Possums* would not be the exact phrase that Rick would describe Mary's movement. She was moving more like a buoy, floating in the harbor on a quiet evening, swaying back and forth to the even tempo of the waves. Now Rick had one more item of mind-candy to get him through the next long week in the Army. Mary stood at the counter in front of him and put both her elbows down on the shiny surface. Resting her chin in her hands, she leaned over so her face was directly in front of Rick's.

"So, Rick, I am ready to get out of here whenever your carriage arrives."

"Maybe we should get out of here now before I cause some real damage."

"Good point." Mary turned her head and yelled back to the long window in the back of the counter. "Uncle Bob, I am going now."

"Have a good time," The window yelled back. "See you tomorrow morning."

Rick did not jump up from his stool but sat there a moment and watched Mary walk around the end of the counter again. She was moving faster now, so her long brown hair was doing a flowing bounce, only tickling her shoulders every other step. Snapping out of his hypnotic state, Rick got up quickly and met her at the front door.

"Lead me to your carriage, kind sir," Mary said and grabbed Rick's upper arm with both of her hands as they walked through the diner door.

"Well, here is your carriage, young maiden," Rick said as he led Mary up to his Jeep.

"I love Jeeps," Mary said with evident excitement in her voice. "You don't see many of them around here."

"I would think this would be good Jeep country with all the wild swamps and back roads."

"I know, but there are not many, and yellow, I love yellow. And it looks like new."

"That's because it is. It is only six months old. It is my, getting out of the Army gift, to myself."

Rick had the doors off, so when he grabbed Mary's hand to help her step up into the Jeep, he was able to turn a potentially awkward move into a very smooth one.

"Thank you, sir, you have helped ladies into carriages before, haven't you?"

Rick just smiled, walked around to the other side, and hopped into the driver's seat.

"Ok, Mary, you need to put on your seat belt. This is a Jeep, you know, with no doors."

"Yes, sir, captain," Mary said as she saluted with her left hand and buckled up with her right.

"You know that would get you fifty pushups in the army."

"What?"

"Saluting with your left hand like that."

"You're kidding?"

"No, I am not, and I will expect those fifty when we get to your house."

"Yes, sir," Mary said as she saluted with her left hand again." Sorry, that means I owe you one hundred pushups, doesn't it?"

"My God, you are not only good-looking, but you are a math whiz also."

"I study very hard at it."

"Ok, which way to your house?"

"We are about five miles away, so that will give you some time to get ready for my parents."

"Ready for your parents? Is there something that you are not telling me?"

"Oh, not really, they are sort of, a little protective, if you know what I mean."

"You mean like they give all your men callers the first-degree?"

"Yea, something like that, but you will do just fine. My dad was in the Army in World War II, so I would assume he will get along with you."

"I should not be concerned about a shotgun or anything, should I?"

"No, silly," After a short pause, Mary continued, "he only uses an ax."

"Oh, that's much better."

"I am just kidding," Mary said as she touched Rick gently on the arm, "You will do just fine. And I am sure you cannot do any worse than the last ten guys who came to my house with me. Of course, three of them are still missing out in the swamps somewhere."

"Very funny, maybe I should wait in the car with the engine running."

"No, my parents are really ok, really."

"I will take your word for it, but if your dad excuses himself to go chop some wood, I am out of there."

"Trust me, if that happens, we both will be out of there."

They were both laughing as they pulled into Mary's driveway.

Mary's house was at the end of a short, narrow drive off the main highway. Along the sides of the driveway was a scattering of downed and broken trees. The spaces between were filled with a thick underbrush of twisted twigs and branches. The white sand was sprinkled with long green sprigs of Sand Spur vines, giving the whole drive a jungle feeling. The small cinder block house, with a coating of very white paint, was like an oasis in the scruff woodland. Its sandy landscape was well kept, with large, pruned hedges on each side of the front door. The overall symmetry was broken by an out-of-place double car garage off to one side. The orderliness was also shattered by two old, junked cars that were nestled close to the garage. Above the garage looked like an apartment of some sort. Rick pulled the Jeep into the drive and parked behind one of the old cars that, obviously, was not going anywhere. After stopping the Jeep, he got out and quickly moved around to Mary's side. The drop from the Jeep was a long one, so Rick gently held Mary's hand and guided her down to the ground.

"Thank you, kind sir. You certainly are one of those rare gentlemen, aren't you"?

Rick started to release his grip on Mary's hand, but she held on and slowly led him down a broken sidewalk to the front door of the house.

Mary opened the door with her free hand, and as she continued to lead Rick into the house, she yelled with a loud voice, "Mom, Dad, I'm home."

"Were out in the back dear," a kind-sounding women's voice echoed through the house.

Letting go of Rick's hand, Mary said, "Why don't you wait here a second, and I will see what they are up to."

Rick watched Mary go through the open doorway and out into the back yard where she gave each of her parents a big hug and kiss.

This is one close family, Rick thought. *I don't think I ever hugged my parents, let alone gave them a kiss.*

26

Before Rick could dwell too much more on his family's lack of affection, Mary came into the room dragging her father by the hand. Not unlike the way she had pulled him into the house.

"Rick, this is my dad, Carl," Mary said as she pushed her dad's hand towards Rick, forcing a handshake.

Carl reluctantly reached out his hand and shook Rick's with a very firm and authoritative grip.

"How do you do there, young man?"

"Fine sir, I...."

Before Rick could finish, Mary's mother came into the room, and Mary ran over to her and dragged her over to Rick.

"This is Rick, Mom."

"Glad to meet you." Her mother said as she extended her hand out to Rick.

Rick shook her hand lightly and said, "It is a pleasure, ma'am."

Before Rick could continue, Mary's father interrupted, "Where are you two going tonight?"

Mary answered very quickly, "Rick said he wanted to take me out to a movie."

"I hear you are a soldier," Mary's father asked without paying attention to what Mary had said about a movie.

"Yes, sir, I am. Soon to be a former soldier. I get discharged at the end of the summer."

"I see," Mary's father said without much emotion.

"Rick, can you wait a few minutes here while I go change," Mary said as she started towards the back of the house. "Unless you want me to keep on this stylish pink uniform."

Rick was going to answer with a smart-ass comment on how sexy he thought she looked in her pink uniform, but wisely did not say anything.

"Sure, no problem," Rick answered with an uncomfortable voice.

As Mary turned and walked down the hallway, he had a tough time not watching the movement of her pink uniform again. He thought it best to keep eye contact with the father.

"You can sit over here, young man." Mary's father said as he motioned to an old cloth-covered couch.

"Thank you," Rick said as he sat down.

"So, what are you planning to do with your life after you get out of the army?"

"Oh, I don't know. I guess I have just been thinking about getting out and not had much time to think about what I am going to do."

"I was in World War II, you know, the Italian campaign."

"That was probably a tough one, wasn't it?"

"Yes, it was, and you?

"Oh, I was drafted and have just been playing soldier."

"Playing soldier? It sounds like you do not care for military life that much."

"Actually, I pretty much hate everything about it."

"I see. Did you go to Vietnam?"

"Yes, I did."

After a long pause, Carl said. "Enough said."

It was apparent that neither one of them wanted to talk about either.

After another long pause, Carl said, "Ok, you two have a nice time tonight and make sure you bring Mary home early."

"Yes, sir."

Carl then got up and left the room without saying another word. Rick knew it was an abrupt exit, but he was very used to this kind of behavior with all the anti-soldier movements going around. Rick was surprised that a former soldier would have such an attitude, however. Rick sat on the oversized couch, alone in the room.

"That went well," he said in a low mumble. He meant to just think it, but it came out seemly all by itself. He had a feeling that Mary was not kidding about what she had said about her parents. It was pretty evident that Mary's father disapproved of him going out with his daughter. He was hoping he was not going to get an ax.

Mary's mother came into the room shortly after Carl left and sat down next to Rick.

"Can I get you anything?"

"No thanks, I'm fine."

"I'm sorry if Carl seemed a little rude leaving you alone out here, but he is very protective of his only daughter, you know."

"That's ok, but I did get the impression that he was not too happy with me."

"Oh, that could be, but don't take it personally, as he is not happy with anyone that goes out with his daughter. And you being a soldier, probably did not help your case much. He was a soldier also, you know."

"Yes, he told me."

"You and Mary did just meet, you know, so you cannot blame him too much. You seem like a nice boy, but I will show my concerns if I have to."

Rick knew that was her way of saying, *you better be nice to my daughter.*

"You two have a nice time, and I would bring Mary home early to keep Carl happy, and me, of course."

"Yes, ma'am, I will."

Mary's mother smiled, and before anything else could be said, Mary walked into the room. She had changed her pink uniform into a short skirt and a frilly white blouse with most of her neck showing.

"You look very nice," Rick said. He was thinking, however, that she looked lovely. Beautiful, with a radiance that made him forget all about her parents' negative feelings hanging over the room.

Mary said quietly, "Bye, Mom." Turning her head away from her mother, she yelled towards the back of the house, "Dad, I am going now."

"Be home early," Carl replied from the back of the house.

"I will."

"It was nice meeting you." her mother said to Rick as Mary grabbed Rick's hand and led him out the door. Just like she had done what seemed like hours earlier.

When they had settled into the Jeep, Mary reached over and held Rick's hand and said, "I hope that was not too tough for you in there. I know that my parents can be a little intimidating at times with the men in my life. They are very protective of their only daughter, you know."

"Oh, it was fine. I have had worse. Well, maybe not."

Pulling her hand away from Rick's, Mary said, "I hope you don't mind, but I picked out a movie for us to see."

"No, that's fine. What is it?"

"It is called *Young Frankenstein.* A comedy with Gene Wilder."

"Good choice, I heard about it. Isn't Terri Garr in there also? I really like her."

"I bet you do," Mary said as she slugged Rick on the shoulder.

The glow around Mary radiated as she pulled back from Rick's arm and reached over and touched Rick's hand that was resting on the gear-shift knob. A surge of excitement flashed through Rick's body from her simple touch. This was a feeling that Rick had not experienced in a very long time, and he was not exactly sure how he was going to handle it. He managed as they drove off.

Rick and Mary truly enjoyed the movie. They both laughed until they cried. Rick was uncertain if the film was the focus or something going on between him and Mary. Or it could have very well been the fact that Mary insisted on holding his hand during the entire movie. The movie got over later than expected. Even though it was not that late, Rick took Mary directly home to avoid a clash with Mary's parents. Once in Mary's drive, Rick felt a little more comfortable, as he felt like he had fulfilled his home-early obligation. Rick again hurried around to Mary's door, grabbed her hand, and helped her out of the Jeep. It was a grip that stayed long after her feet were planted firmly on the ground. They held hands all the way to Mary's front door. Still holding Mary's hand, Rick grabbed the screen door handle to open it for her.

"Nice knocker," said Mary, laughing out loud.

"You took that movie way too seriously," said Rick.

"And you took Terri Garr's knockers way too serious."

"I suppose I did."

Still holding hands at the front door, Mary pulled Rick close and said in a soft voice, "I had a great time tonight. You are a very nice person to be around."

"Thank you, it was a nice night, wasn't it? Even with the cold reception with your parents."

"Oh, it was not that bad."

"Yes, I know it wasn't"

With a brief look into each other's eyes, Rick pulled her closer, and they exchanged a short, good-night kiss. It was a quick kiss, but Rick felt an excitement that he had felt only a few times in his life. An excitement that was as rare as feelings could get. By the look in Mary's eyes, he knew that Mary was feeling it also.

After a long pause and a long exchange of glances, Mary broke the silence with a "so, are you going to be around tomorrow night?"

"Well, I thought I might stick around here for a while since I drove five hours to get here."

After another long pause, Mary asked in a joking tone, "Do you have anything planned?"

"No, did you want to do something?"

"Well, I forgot that I have to go with my parents to this annual dance. Sorry, but I forgot all about it. We have all been going to this thing for as long as I can remember."

After a short pause, Mary said," Would you like to come along? I would really enjoy it if you did. It is really sort of boring, but with you there, it could actually be fun."

"Your parents wouldn't mind?"

"Oh, I don't think so, but they are still up. Should we go ask?"

Before Rick could answer, Mary kept hold of his hand, led him through the front door and into the living room. Mary's mother and father were sitting on the couch and barely looked up when they entered the room. Mary interrupted them in whatever they were doing and forced their attention.

With an excited tone, Mary asked," Mom, Dad, is it alright if Rick goes to the dance with us tomorrow night?" Without giving them a chance to answer, she continued." It would sure make it more fun for me."

Mary's dad answered back almost immediately, "Sure, that would be fine, but I am sure that this young man has little interest in our old music and our old dance steps."

Rick could tell by his tone that he was trying to discourage him from going.

"What kind of dance is it, sir?" Rick asked with a sincere and respectful tone in his voice.

"You probably have never heard of our Big Band Era, have you? Back when bands played real music with a melody."

Rick didn't say anything.

"I didn't think so. Glenn Miller, Tommy Dorsey, do these guys sound familiar to you? Glenn Miller started his band from scratch in the thirties, and if that plane crash had not got him, he would still be more popular than any Beatle. What do you think about that, son?"

32

"Well, I."

Before Rick could finish, Mary's dad started again. "I just don't see how you kids can listen to that noise that you call music today."

"Carl," Mary's mother interrupted, "You have said your piece, and we all know how you feel." Turning to Rick, Mary's mother said, "You are more than welcome to come along with us if you would like to."

Rick heard a low grumble from Mary's father, which everyone ignored.

It was apparent that Mary's father was trying to discourage Rick from going along with the family. It would have taken a lot more than his negativity to keep Rick from being with Mary this weekend.

Just as Mary's father started to get up and leave the room, Rick spoke towards his back. "I really do know something about the Big Band Era."

Mary's father turned for a moment just to be polite. "Is that so, and what can you tell me about it?"

"Actually sir, Glenn Miller helped the Dorsey brothers started their band in 1934, and it was not until 1937 that Glenn Miller started his own band. By 1939 he was all over the charts with hit records. I wish he had not gotten on that plane at the end of the war. Who knows what kind of great sounds he would have come up with"?

Mary's dad has now turned entirely around, facing Rick with a look of surprise on his face. After a long pause with just looking at Rick, he said, "And may I ask just how you know so much about Glen Miller and swing bands?"

Rick thought for a long moment about whether he should say any more or not, as he knew he had already said too much. "Actually, I sang with a big-band for a while back in college."

Now both Mary and her father were looking at Rick with equal looks of disbelief mixed with shock. Now a very long pause filled

33

the room. Broken only by Mary's father saying," Is that so."
Then he added, with a sadistic grin on his face, "Well, since
you are such a big fan of our music, maybe you should go with
us tomorrow night."

Mary snapped out of her stunned look long enough to add,
"That will be great, won't it, Rick?"

Not waiting for an answer, she grabbed Rick's hand, pulled
him away from her father, and out the front door. She walked at
a fast pace all the way to Rick's Jeep.

When they reached the Jeep, Mary immediately turned to
Rick, still holding his hand, and said with a slightly raised
voice," why did you tell my father that you sang in a big-band?
He takes his dancing and music very seriously, you know. You
didn't really sing with a big-band, did you?"

"Why does it matter?"

"It matters because my father is a sincere and honest man.
He would not tolerate anything else. It would also be the
perfect excuse for him to not let me see you anymore. So, were
you serious in there? Were you really a singer?"

There was another long pause before Rick answered. "I am
pretty honest myself, you know, and I don't tell stories."
Another pause. "Yes, I really did sing with a band back in
college, although I know your father does not believe me."

"Yes, I know," Mary said as she put her arms around Rick's
neck. With a big smile and an unmistakable look of relief, she
continued," I have to admit that I did have my doubt for a
moment there. Sorry for being so harsh."

"You're forgiven."

With her arms still around Rick's neck, Mary said, "So why
don't you come by around six tomorrow night, and we can all
go together to the dance."

"Great," Rick said with forced enthusiasm.

Mary reached up on her toes and gave Rick a nice good
night kiss on his cheek, followed by a "thank you."

"Thank you, for what?" Rick asked.

"Oh, just thank you. Really, it will be fun tomorrow, even with my parents."

"Right," Rick replied with doubt in his voice." It will be great, ballroom dance with a bunch of gray-haired people and two parents, one of which would love to go chop wood with me." After a short pause and as he looked into Mary's beautiful brown eyes. Rick continued, "It will be awfully nice being with you tomorrow, and I am glad we are going, really."

Not having let go of Rick's neck, Mary pulled him down to her five-foot four-level and gave him a kiss on the lips. It was not a passionate kiss, but it was a long kiss. Rick let go of Mary's hand with a slight final squeeze and climbed up into his Jeep. He waved to Mary as he left for his Holiday Inn barracks.

Rick woke up just as the sun was coming up. Another lifelong curse that the Army had bestowed on him. He immediately put on his running shorts, an old tee shirt with ragged edges where the arms had been cut out, and a pair of running shoes. Without much else of a morning ritual, he started the beginning of his three-mile run. His morning runs were one of the positive routines that the Army had given him. The 0600 hour air was crisp, even with the Florida sun already heating up in the cloudless sky. Running for Rick was when he got some of his best thinking in. It was his time to reflect on things that required a deep concentration. This concentration automatically took the pain away from his burning muscles. This morning his thoughts, of course, were all about Mary. His thoughts were that he would love to be with her at that moment.

She was working at her uncle's diner, which precluded this. It was difficult but, in a way, was a good thing. Rick had learned from experience that too much togetherness at the beginning of a relationship creates unneeded awkwardness. An awkwardness that creates problems. He really liked this lady, and he wanted not to have these kinds of early issues to keep them from a potentially wonderful time together. They were not together, but they might as well have been, as she had been in his thoughts since they met.

Rick returned to his hotel, showered, got in his Jeep, and drove out of town. You would have thought that he had enough driving under his belt after five hours from Augusta, but he loved it. Rick traveled east of town on highway 90. He traveled to the Osceola National Forest, a nature reserve, where you could drive throughout the park on old dirt roads. Rick drove on many of the back roads through unique original pine tree forests. The tallest pine trees he had seen in Florida.

Being a lover of history, he had to stop at the site of the Olustee Battlefield. He walked a trail through the historic battlefield where 3000 men had died during a fight between Union soldiers and Rebel troops. 10,000 soldiers from both sides entered the tall pine trees and fought a long and drawn-out battle. It was very haunting to Rick, especially with him still in the Army and the whole Vietnam War thing. The thoughts rushed through him of all the many friends that he had lost on those battlefields. He felt the presents of the fallen soldiers at Olustee. With all of that rushing through his head, he had to leave. He returned to his Holiday Inn barracks and took a short rest. It was a great adventure, but he was now ready to see Mary again. He awoke from his nap, took a long shower, and prepared himself to see Mary and face her parents.

CHAPTER 4
The Band

Rick asked Mary if there was a long way to drive to the dance so they could arrive a little later. The thought of having to sit around and make small talk with her parents was not a pleasant thought. Mary agreed, so they drove around the town of Lake City. Mary showed Rick all her old hangouts from a small child to her high school years. Mary really enjoyed showing Rick her past, and Rick truly enjoyed seeing it. Seeing other people's history was always an exciting thing for Rick. Every person was so different, and with all the varieties of backgrounds, it was always amazing how people turn out the way they do. They stopped and talked at every one of Mary's historical spots, so time slipped away. By the time they arrived at the dance hall, there were very few parking spaces left. Ironically, the only spot they could find was right next to a 1962 green Cadillac. Yes, it was Mary's parent's car.

"What are the odds?" Rick said. Turning his head towards Mary, just enough so she could see him roll his eyes.

"Must be a fate thing," said Mary

"I guess, or your dad has more clout with the parking gods than we think. Or your dad reserved the spot just for us so he could keep a closer eye on you. So much for leaving early now."

Rick pulled into the empty spot, turned off the ignition, and gave Mary a look. Over the top of his eyelids.

"All right then, here we go."

He lunged out of his door with a quick motion and rushed around to Mary's side of the Jeep. The doors and top were still off the Jeep, so it was easy to reach and offer his hand to Mary.

"My lady, may I escort you to the ball"

"Why yes, you may, kind sir, you are quite the gentleman you know."

"We will see what your parents have to say about that before the evening is finished."

Rick guided Mary out of the Jeep with a firm grip. She then pretended to lose her balance and fell into Rick's helpful arms. Creating a nice moment for a healthy hug and a warm kiss.

"I must warn you," Rick said, we must leave before the stroke of midnight, or this Jeep will turn into a pumpkin and the engine into little white mice."

"We cannot have that," said Mary, "and just what do you turn into?"

"Oh, just a frog."

They both laughed.

Rick started to let go of Mary's hand, but she tightened her grip just enough to tell him that she enjoyed precisely where it was. Rick was happy to oblige her.

"Ok, let's get this over with, my dear," said Rick.

They slowly walked towards the large dance hall, snaking their way in and out of the parked cars.

The building was a straightforward design, looking more like a giant factory than a dance hall. There was no visible sign of any windows. The multi-layers of paint hid the fact that it was all cinder block construction. The dull gray color added to the industrial look.

"Now, this really looks like a hot nightspot." Rick mumbled with a sarcastic tone, "Your parents do know how to party."

"Oh, come on now, be nice. It is very functional."

"Sorry, but I didn't know if we were coming here to dance or process sugar cane."

Mary lightly jerked Rick's arm, just enough to toss him off balance and miss a step.

As they got closer to the large glass double doors, something like you would see at the local supermarket, the sounds of musical instruments came flowing out into the night air. Flowing is probably an oversimplification, as each instrument seemed to be playing something different. Obviously, the band was starting to warm up. Rick opened one of the large glass doors for Mary to walk in ahead of him. The open door increased the volume of the instrument by a factor of ten.

"Wow," said Rick looking up at the high ceiling that rose above them. "we're not in a sugar factory anymore, are we?"

The ceiling extended almost as far as could be seen, and with it painted black above the cross beams, it looked like it was out in the night sky.

"This is like walking into a baseball stadium," Rick said, still looking up at the high ceiling.

Rick's hypnotic state was interrupted when he heard a loud "Mary" from the other side of the large room. Mary gave a quick wave. Still holding onto Rick's hand, she started leading him across the room at a swift pace. They were weaving in and out of tables with hips barely clearing their edges. Rick's foot caught on a chair leg, and he had to do a quick hop to keep from tumbling to the ground. Mary did not break her stride. Rick thought it reminded him of a horse running back to a barn after a long ride, but he decided to keep that to himself.

Finally, at the table, Mary's mother gave her a warm hug and offered her hand to Rick with a big smile. Rick gently grabbed it and returned the smile. Her hand seemed small and almost fragile but very warm.

"So glad you two could make it," she said, still holding on to Rick's hand.

Mary's dad halfway stood up from the table. He offered Rick an obligatory handshake that was extremely firm; firm, almost to the point of being intimidating. Rick just squeezed slightly and smiled.

"Good to see you, sir," Rick said with the same smile still on his face. A semi grunt came from Mary's dad.

"This is a very nice place you have here, sir, exquisite. You sure would not guess it from the outside of the building."

"We like it," Mary's dad answered back as he sat back down.

As Mary started sitting down, Rick quickly moved behind her chair and gently slipped it under her. He was being polite, but it was mainly to try and impress her parents. No one noticed.

Rick had just sat down when the waitress came by, asking Mary if she cared for anything to drink. Mary just said, "A Coke, please."

"And you, sir?" The waitress asked.

Rick paused as he really thought that he could use a very stiff drink.

"Coke will be fine," he said while trying very hard not to look over at Mary's father. Rick knew he was watching him order a drink very closely. A few seconds afterward, he sneaked a quick glance at him. He was sipping on an iced bourbon and water. Rick could taste it.

"Did you two have any trouble finding a parking spot?" Mary's mother asked.

"Not at all," Mary said. "We actually found one right next to the Cadillac."

"My Jeep and your Cadillac look very well together out there," Rick said, trying to keep the small talk flowing.

"I bet," said Mary's mother, "like a city mouse and a country mouse."

"That was a good one," Rick said.

Mary and Rick did a very polite laugh while Mary's dad took another drink of his bourbon and water.

Rick escaped the conversation by looking around the room at the fantastic decorations and the vastness of the place. The wood dance floor was as large as a tennis court. At each side of the dance floor were the tables. There had to be at least fifty, each with a candle at the center. The tables were starting to fill with an ocean of mostly gray heads. These gray heads were all bobbing to a flow of conversations. They were all drinking what looked like many alcoholic beverages, from cone-shaped martini glasses to classic wine glasses.

At the far side of the dance floor was a band platform; a large stage that rose at least a foot above the dance floor. There were at least twenty chairs, each sitting behind a large cardboard plate. The cardboard plate hid much of the bottom of the chair. Stenciled in fancy graphics on the cardboard were the initials PH, which Rick assumed was the band leader's name. A series of standing microphones were in front of and off to the side of the herd of chairs. Six mics were lined up in a straight line, obviously for the backup singers. In front of the backup mics, there were two microphones spaced about 6 feet apart. Rick figured that these were for the lead singers. Out of the corner of his eye, he noticed a woman walking across the dance floor from the bandstand. She was coming in the direction of their table.

She was a towering woman, on the front side of six feet. Her hair was a light black, short, and formed with the old Doris Day flip look. Her face stayed with the same Doris Day theme. bright eyes, a confident bouncing step, and a smile that stretched all the way across her face. She walked with a grace that could only have come out of the Big Band Era. A long black gown tightly embraced her slender body. A body that had obviously traveled a great distance in time but still retained the form of a young woman. A single strap hung on her right shoulder while the other shoulder was bare and exposed to the air around it.

Mary's mother was the first to see her.

41

"So nice to see you," she said as she singled out Mary's mother at the far end of the table.

"Linda how are you?" she said as she jumped up from the table and greeted her with a big hug. A hug that she had to reach up high for, as this woman in black was so much taller.

"And Carl, you old coot, how are you doing?"

Carl just said, "Hello, Linda."

"You remember Mary," Joyce said as she motioned with her outstretched hand for Mary to stand up. Rick stood up with Mary, and they both walked over to Linda, where Mary got a very hard hug.

"My, you have turned into a fine-looking young woman. I bet you are fighting off all the boys with a big willow branch, or is your dad doing that for you?"

Mary did not answer but shot an embarrassed grin over at Rick.

"And who is this fine-looking young man next to you?" Linda said as she stretched out her hand and grabbed Rick's, catching him off guard enough to pull him in for a nice friendly hug.

Mary, embarrassed again, blurted out, "This is Rick, a friend of mine."

"Well, glad to meet you, Rick. Mary, you know he is a nice-looking keeper, don't you?" Grinning, she then asked, "Ever been to Casablanca?"

There was a long pause as Rick searched for a creative, Humphrey Bogart answer. None came.

As Linda was eyeing Rick and waiting for him to answer. Carl interrupted the conversation with a loud, "You know this boy here has claimed that he has sung with a big-band a few times. I bet you could always use another voice up there, couldn't you?"

"Well, we are short a few backup singers tonight, but we could not ask this poor guy to help us out."

"Of course, you could," said Carl with a sadistic, evil tone. "I bet he would love to get up there and sing with you people. Wouldn't you, Rick?"

"I guess so," said Rick with a surprised and reluctant tone.

"Are you sure, young man?" said Linda.

Rick put his shoulders back with renewed confidence and spoke. "It would be great to sing again, but don't count on me being in tune right away. It has been a while."

"Don't worry," said Linda, with an excitement in her voice. "We always look out for each other. Plus, you are probably better than most of my old fart singers who like to hit the bottle a little too much."

Linda stretched out her hand for Rick to grab. "Come on then, let's see if we can find you something to wear and look over some music."

Before Rick knew what was happening, Linda took his hand with a firm grip and started to drag him across the dance floor towards the stage. Rick felt like a little kid being towed through the supermarket by his mother. He did have time to turn and give a quick look back at Mary, who just shrugged her shoulders and lipped the words, "Sorry."

Linda's long legs were moving so fast that Rick had difficulty keeping up with her, especially since she was still holding on to his hand. Linda jumped up on the foot-high stage with the ease of a gazelle while Rick had to struggle with a clumsy hop. If Linda had not been hanging onto him, he would have done a face plant onto the hardwood. She finally slowed down when they came to a large red curtain at the back of the stage. The curtain extended the entire length of the stage and went from the stage floor into the darkness of the high ceiling. A scruffy old guy was meticulously arranging chairs and music stands off to the right, where the band would be sitting.

"That is our conductor," Linda whispered in a low tone. "Hey Phil, I found us another voice for tonight. Phil, this is Rick."

43

"Can he sing?" Phil yelled with a smirk on his face.

"I don't know," said Linda. "I guess we'll find out."

"Welcome aboard, kid, sing or not, we just need warm bodies up there that can move their lips."

Rick did the best laugh he could come up with and said, "Good to meet you, sir."

Before Phil could answer back, Rick felt his hand jerk again, and they were heading for the big curtain. How Linda found the opening was a mystery, but she did and flung it open wide enough for the two of them to fit through. Behind the curtain was another world. A large area was littered with musical instrument cases, some closed, others wide open. Scattered around the place were, maybe, twenty musicians. Each one was in their own little world making love to their individual instruments. They were tuning, blowing, plucking, slapping, twisting, licking, strumming, and sliding. They all were doing whatever was necessary for them to contribute their part to the band.

"Hey everyone, this is Rick, and he'll be helping us out with vocals tonight."

Everyone looked up, and many said, "Welcome, Rick," but it was short-lived as they all returned to their musical tasks.

Linda never let go of her firm grip on Rick's hand and pulled him farther back into the stage. A large round table in the middle of the room was covered with sheet music and various cocktail glasses. At the back of the table was a large chalkboard with song titles written on it in little boxes and many arrows going from one to the other. Three ladies and two guys were sitting at the table. They were all dressed in black and were all older, around Linda's age, early 50's maybe. They were all so deep in conversations that they did not notice Rick and Linda walk up.

"Hey, you guys, this is Rick, and he is going to give us another badly needed male voice this evening."

"Wonderful," said the short red-haired lady as she got up and extended out her hand to Rick.

"Hi Rick, I'm Barb," Holding on to Rick's hand, she walked him around the table, introducing him to each of the other singers.

"This is Cathy, Carol, Ron, and Bob," Each shook Rick's hand, and then all sat back down to continue talking about the show.

Bob stayed standing and said, "Glad to have you with us, Rick. We really needed another male voice. When Linda and Ron are out front, it is pretty lonely out there at the lower end of the voice scale."

"I bet," Rick answered back. "Three to one, I bet you probably get drowned out pretty good."

"Sure do," Bob continued with an inquisitive tone. "Have you done much of this stuff?"

"I sang with a big-band in college, but that was a long time ago. I can surely fake it if I have to."

"Great," said Bob, "we all do that anyway."

Still holding on to Rick's hand and slapping him on the shoulder with his other, he led Rick farther back into the stage.

"Let's see if we can find you something to wear back here."

A long clothes rack of black coats, pants, and gowns mixed with some white shirts and ties was off to the side.

"Fortunately, you look like a standard size, a 42 regular, I bet. Here's one right here. Why don't you try it on and come out and join us? We're on in 30 minutes, so we have some work to do.

"Thanks."

"Oh," Bob pulled out of his pocket a silver flask. "Here, this will help you get started."

Rick took a big swig of the bourbon nectar inside, "Thanks Bob, I needed that."

"You had that look like you did, my friend."

The black coat and pants were a little small, but they would do. *Pretty fancy*, Rick thought. The only dress clothes that he had worn in the past three years was his dress uniform. The black was much nicer than that ugly Army green.

As soon as Rick appeared back at the table, Linda handed him a music sheet book with all the songs for the evening.

"My, don't you look a handsome young man."

Opening the book for him, Linda questioned, "You do read music, don't you, dear?"

"Yes, I do, and I will know when to come in and fade out if that is what you are worried about."

"I figured I had better ask. It would be complicated if you didn't. I suppose I should have asked before you got all dressed up." She said with a nervous laugh. Just do what you feel comfortable with, and the rest you can just fake. Although with just you and Bob back there, faking it is going to be a little more complicated."

"You could have left that last thing out," Rick said.

"Ron and I do the lead singing, so all you have to do is sing backup, and it is all right there in front of you."

Rick looked over the songs. There were only around six of them.

"Good thing you guys do these classics," said Rick, "I've done all of these at one time or another. It was a few lifetimes ago, however."

"That is a relief," said Linda. "I was starting to get a little worried. Only a little, but worried. Just remember, we are not playing Carnegie Hall. We are in the middle of the Florida swamps." They both laughed.

Linda paused and, with a smirk, said, "And it is a tough job trying to impress your date, isn't it?"

"And her grumpy father," Rick mumbled under his breath. Not wanting Linda to hear it, but she did.

"I hear you, Carl is a piece of work, but he really is a nice guy once you get to know him.

And Mary is a real sweetie, so it will be worth it."

After a slight pause, she added, "If you pull this off, that is."

"Thanks a lot. You did it again. You should have stopped at; it will be worth it."

They laughed again.

"Ok, everyone, we have time to run through some of these songs for Rick here. Be gentle on him," Linda said with a wink in Rick's direction.

Ron and Linda's voices were so strong that they could almost get by without backup singers.

"Well, That's All Right" was the first song, and Rick was glad as all the backup singers had to do was say, "we'll, all right" at specific points.

"Tuxedo Junction" was another easy one for Rick as he had played it on the piano for years. Usually, it was played mainly by the band. This band had some simple vocals tossed in.

"Don't Sit Under the Apple Tree" was another good one, and Rick had done it many times. It was tricky as there were so many different voices and strange places to come in. But all the singers were doing it together, so it would endure minor mistakes.

"Chattanooga Choo Choo" was a tough one as there would be many places where a screw-up would be obvious. It was one of Rick's favorite tunes to sing, and he had done it probably more than any of the others. It was so much fun to do if it came together right.

"Moonlight Cocktail" was another tough one with lots of voices. Ron was singing lead by himself, so everyone else was back up, including Linda's strong voice.

"Till Then" was the finish. A wonderful song that Rick loved dearly for its meaning during the war years. Ron and Linda would be doing the lead, so backups were just a lot of "humming" and "who-haas." What a wonderful song to finish with. Fortunately, these were all classics that Rick had sung before. It was way back in college, but he felt very confident after singing during the practice. Linda had mentioned earlier that it would be just like

47

riding a bike, and it was. He had forgotten how much fun it was to sing with a group like this. Back in college, he only joined the swing band at the request of the piano player. His main incentive for joining the band was not to sing but to get into the piano player's pants. Diane was a beauty, and could she play that piano. It all worked, as they became an item right after he joined the band. It was a blast playing for all the old folks. News Years and Valentine dances were the best. They were always packed, and everyone had so much fun dancing to their music. The best was when Diane and Rick were on a break, sitting at a table on the dance floor. They would constantly be surrounded by groups of old people. They wanted to talk with them about the old days and give them endless compliments. The main praise was, "It is so nice that you young people are playing and enjoying our music." The old men would shake Rick's hand and give Diane a hug. Then they would buy them drinks. The old women would hug both. Such good memories of those band days.

Wonder how Diane is doing? Rick thought.

Rick's thoughts did not last long as Phil, the conductor, yelled, "Ok, people, let's do this. We will do one last tune-up on stage and get this show on the road."

Now Rick's stomach was doing the butterfly shuffle. *What the hell are you doing?*

In a low, almost whispering voice, Linda said, "We don't go out until our first song is up, then we come back here and wait for the next vocal. We have found it is better than standing out there and looking stupid." She laughed.

The band filed out and sat in their appropriate spots. They did a final tune-up, filled with squeaks, squawks, and toots. Instantly, Phil appeared on his stand, and with a quick tap of his baton, "In the Mood" started playing.

A cheer came from the crowd. Immediately, couples were flowing out of the shadows and onto the dance floor. The lights hit the dance floor, and for the first time, Rick saw how enormous the place really was. The biggest shock was seeing how many people were there. There had to be more than 300 bodies. The butterflies started fluttering again.

Towards the end of "In the Mood", Ron and Linda started walking out the curtain. They stopped at the two microphones in front of the band. Barb grabbed Rick's hand and started pulling him out on the stage. "Let's go, honey. This will be a piece of cake."

Bob, Cathy, and Carol followed close behind.

The backup singers had their own microphones in the back of Ron and Linda but off to the side. The ladies went in line first, followed by Rick and Bob, who were at the end. Fortunately for Rick, the stage lights were such that he could not see the people in the audience, especially Mary and her parents. He was happy about that as he really did not want to see them while on stage.

The band finished "In the Mood", and after a short time, they jumped right into the next song. "Well, That's All Right." "we'll all right," were the only words that the backup singers had to sing about a dozen times. It was a piece of cake. Rick sighed a little relief, and the butterflies had flown away for the time being.

"Tuxedo Junction" came right away, and it also was easy for the backups. The song was a new arrangement for Rick, but he knew it so well that it worked out well.

The band played "Little Brown Jug".

"Don't Sit Under the Apple Tree" followed. Linda and Ron did most of the singing on this one. Backups just did some echoing.

The band played "Indian Summer", which was all instrumental, so Rick and all the singers left. Backstage, Bob gave some tips on the next song as the two of them were the only ones doing the backup. The women were not in it. Of course, there was another swig from his flask.

Towards the end of "Moonlight Serenade", another instrumental, all the singers walked out to their mics. The intro to

"Moonlight Cocktail" started. Rick and Bob looked at each other, Bob winked. *These people are so professional and friendly,* Rick thought. The song went better than Rick thought it would and was not as complicated as he thought. He was enjoying the excitement of the singing so much that he was surprised when it was intermission.

Rick did not really want to go out and face Carl, but before he could think any more about it, Linda grabbed his hand. "Let's go, son, and get out there and see how our Mary is doing."

She once again quickly led him through the big curtain, across the stage, and out onto the dance floor.

Here we go again, thought Rick, as he almost tripped down the stage as gracefully as he had come up it. Linda's pace slowed to a crawl as they approached the table. Mary was the first to see them approaching. She gave Rick a wide smile as she stood up and left her table to greet them.

"You guys did great up there," Mary said as she gave Linda a short hug. Then she came over to Rick and, to his shock, gave him a long hug. Grabbing both of their hands, Mary then led them over to her table. Mary's mother got up as soon as she saw them coming and gave Linda and Rick a big hug.

I barely know these people, and they act like I am a long-time friend. Out of the corner of his eye, Rick saw Carl starting to stand up. Linda quickly went over to his side of the table and gave him a hug, which he, uncomfortably, returned. Rick could have sworn he was smiling. He then saw Rick and stretched his hand across the table towards him. Rick shook his hand firmly.

"You did a wonderful job up there, son. I have to say that I am pleasantly surprised and impressed."

"Thank you, sir."

"You and Mary sit down and rest."

"Hey, you," Mary said as she turned Rick around by grabbing his shoulder. "How are you doing?"

"Feeling pretty good," Rick said. "How did we sound up there?"

"Everyone sounded great. I do believe you impressed my dad. He made a lot of nice comments while you were up there. I will tell you later."

"How about my moves?" Mary said, "Giving Linda a big hug so I could give you one. And, holding her hand so I could grab yours without looking too obvious."

"That was brilliant, I have to admit, although I was pretty shocked."

"Shocked?" Mary said as she hit Rick on his upper arm.

"Thrilled, I should have said," Rick quickly answered back.

"That's a little better."

"Ok," Linda spoke up. "We need to be getting back, Ricky, my boy." She grabbed Rick's hand again.

Before Rick could pull his hand away or say anything to Mary, she had it and was once again dragging him across the floor. He kept up this time and saw the step on the stage coming.

The band was already starting to sit down, and backstage, Ron, Bob, Cathy, and Carol were all standing up, looking at the music sheets.

"Here you go, Rick," Bob said as he handed him the music sheets with his flask underneath.

"Thanks again," Rick said as he screwed off the top and took a healthy drink.

Linda brought everyone in close and semi-whispered, "The band will do two numbers, then we are out there for "Chattanooga Choo Choo". Then they will do two more, and we will finish with "Till Then", sound good?"

All agreed, and Rick took another drink from the flask and handed it back to Bob.

"Thanks again, my friend."

After "String of Pearls", the singers all went out on stage. It was one of Rick's favorite instrumentals, so it was nice to follow it.

The band started playing again.

Rick knew right away it was "Chattanooga Choo Choo". *Damn*, he thought, *this song is where the backup singers do the first line.* His thoughts were short-lived as Bob's finger pointed at him and...

Rick and Bob, "Hi there Tex, what you say?"

Before Rick knew it, the song was over, and he felt great. He had been worried about this one, but he did not have to be, as it went very smoothly. Singing with a great group of people really made it.

Finishing off the night with "Till Then" was a great ending for a great evening. The audience seemed very pleased, as was Rick.

By the time Rick changed clothes, tidied up a little, and said goodbyes to everyone, enough time had passed that much of the hall had already cleared out. Mary and her parents were some of the few people left. Mary was the first to see Rick approaching again, jumping up from the table and running to meet him as he hopped off the stage.

"Hey," Rick said, "How are you doing?"

"Wonderful," Mary said. "That was a wonderful show, and I think my dad is going to be much warmer towards you now. You really impressed him. I might not give you a hug or hold your hand this time. Linda is not here as an excuse."

"Hopefully, we will not need an excuse later," said Rick

"You can count on that big fella."

Mary was right. As soon as Mary's dad saw Rick and Mary coming, he not only stood up but walked around the table to greet Rick and shake his hand.

"Again, son, you did a mighty fine job up there. I am sure that the folks in the band appreciated your help."

"It was a pleasure, sir, and I had so much fun doing it. I didn't realize how much I really missed making music."

Mary's dad just smiled, and her mother came over and gave Rick another hug.

Mary's dad interrupted, "Now that you are here, we are going home now. It is past these old folk's bedtime, you know. See you at home soon, Mary." He amplified the "soon" as they both walked away.

"Could we wait a few minutes for them to go ahead? I have had enough awkwardness for one evening," said Rick.

"I fully understand," Mary said as she grabbed and squeezed Rick's hand.

Giving a quick glance at the door and noticing that Mary's parents were gone, he squeezed back.

"There is nothing like that first hand-holding event with someone, is there?" Rick said with a smile.

"You are so right, brother," Mary said as she squeezed Rick's hand a little tighter. "You are not getting romantic on me, are you, Mr. Rick?"

"I would not do such a thing, Miss Mary."

"Ok, then, make sure you don't."

They continued to hold hands on the long walk to Rick's Jeep, and when he was not shifting gears, all the way back to Mary's house.

Still holding hands at Mary's front door, she grabbed Rick's other hand and turned him towards her. Looking directly into his eyes, she said, "My parents asked if you would like to come to Sunday dinner tomorrow. I didn't know what time you had to get back. They said we could eat around noon."

"I would love to come over, and I thought that tonight was going to be it for seeing you. A delightful surprise, indeed."

"I am glad you think so."

Still facing each other and still holding onto each other's hands, Rick said, "You know how I said that that first

hand-holding was the best thing ever? I was wrong."
Rick slowly leaned over close to Mary's lips as Mary
raised up to his. A pause, a look, and they both did that
first major kiss. It was short but very sweet.

They did not move their faces very far away when
Rick said, "Thank you for a wonderful evening, Mary."

"No, thank you for a wonderful evening and for putting up
with my parents. I know that they really appreciated it."

"Better get inside," said Rick. "Don't want to mess up all
those hard-earned points with Carl."

"Ok," said Mary as she tip-toed up and gave Rick another
short kiss.

"Good night." Good night and drive safe. Why don't you
come over a little early tomorrow, about eleven?"

"Sounds good."

Mary went into the house, and Rick drove off to his Holiday
Inn barracks. They both were feeling very warm and close.

Rick got up at his usual 0600-hours and went out for a 3-
mile run, the nasty Army habit again. By the time he had a cup
of coffee and a shower, it was time to pack up and check out.
He got to Mary's house at eleven and she was on the front
porch step waiting for him. Rick had no sooner shut the engine
off and hopped down out of the Jeep when Mary was in front of
him, wrapping her arms around his neck, and giving him a
friendly hug, and kiss.

"Hi, there, stranger, nice of you to drop by. You just could
not get enough of my parents last night, could you."

"You are on to me," said Rick. I didn't know you were going
to be here."

Mary broke the hug loose enough to hit Rick on the
shoulder.

"You need to be nice."

She then grabbed Rick's hand and led him through the front door into the house. Pretty much at the same pace that Linda had pulled him across the dance floor the night before.

"Sure, seems that a lot of women are dragging me around lately."

"You love it."

"I am not complaining."

Mary let go of Rick's hand as they entered the kitchen, where her mother was busy frying something at the stove.

"Rick's here, mother."

Mary's mother turned away from the stove with a spatula still in her hand.

"Hello Rick, so glad you could join us today."

"Mary, could you set the table for me. It is going to be a little while before dinner is ready, Rick. Carl is in the backyard. Why don't you go say hi?"

Say hi, by myself, without Mary, great. Rick thought. "That would be great," he said, as he headed for the back door.

The backyard was not really a backyard but more like an auto graveyard. There were the same two old cars along the wall of the garage, with their hoods open. Off to the other side was a newer, bright green VW Bug with its front and back hoods open. Carl saw Rick coming, so he stepped out from behind the VW. "I'm over here, son."

Rick rushed over with his hand outstretched, "How are you doing, sir?"

"Doing fine except for this darn German car," Carl said as he shook Rick's hand.

"What is wrong with it?"

"First of all, it is all that metric crap, and I refuse to own a single metric tool. It is Mary's car, and it needs some work before she drives it up North."

"It looks like it is pretty new."

"It is, but it might need new brakes and a tune-up. And the clutch is acting funny. Do you know anything about these things, son?"

Rick knew that he was just making conversation and did not expect an answer.

"I have owned two of these, a 63 and a 69. I also raced a Formula Vee around the Florida SCCA circuit when I went to school in Fort Meyers back in 67."

"Formula Vee, what the heck is that?" Carl asked.

"It is a formula race car that has an old 1300cc VW engine in it."

"So, you do know something about these things."

"I have been under them more than I have driven them if that is what you mean."

Carl attempted an almost laugh.

Rick dropped down to the ground and rolled under the front of the car.

"We would have to pop the wheel off to check for sure, but the brakes seem ok. Can we start it up?"

"Sure, the key is in the ignition."

Rick started the engine, put on the emergency brake, put it in first gear, and slowly let out the clutch. Keeping the engine running and in neutral, he went around to the back of the car and feathered the throttle a few times.

"It is missing a little bit, the clutch is slipping, and the emergency brake is not grabbing well. Outside of that, with only 50,000 miles, it is in great shape."

Carl was silent during the whole event. Rick was sensing that he was not highly knowledgeable about cars. He also realized that he got carried away a little and needed to tone things down a little if he wanted to keep on the good side of this man. Didn't want to make him look stupid.

"That sounds like a lot of stuff wrong," Carl said, scratching his head lightly.

"Actually not," Rick said.

After a moment of thinking and a long silence from both, Rick reluctantly said, "You know I do have all the tools to work on one of these things. I would be happy to fix it up for Mary if you would not mind."

"Mind, I would gladly pay you for doing it."

"Pay is not necessary, sir. I would enjoy doing it."

"I don't know. That is a lot to ask of you," Carl muttered in a low tone.

"I don't have duty again next weekend, so I could bring my tools and work on it then."

Before Carl had time to answer, Rick quickly added, "Is there an auto parts store around here?"

"Yes, there's one in town over by the diner."

Rick thought, *shit, what did I just do?*

It was too late as Carl answered, "That would be mighty nice of you, and I know Mary would appreciate it." After another silence, "OK, I would appreciate it also."

"Dinner is on the table, you two." came Mary's voice from the back door.

Carl motioned to Rick, waving his hand like he was throwing an underhanded softball pitch, "After you, son."

Catfish fried in cornmeal, hush puppies, cornbread, and collard greens. Rick's favorite southern meal. He did not remember telling anyone that, but he was not complaining. It was wonderful. Dinner conversation centered around two topics. The VW Bug, of course, as the first thing asked was, "What were you two doing out there?"

When Carl mentioned how Rick offered to come down the next weekend to work on the car, Rick could see out of the corner of his eye that Mary had a huge grin on her face. She did manage to hide the emotion very well. The rest of the conversation was about the night before. The music, the band, and Rick's singing. Which lead to some talk with Carl about the Glen Miller band and other Big Band groups. Fortunately, Rick was very knowledgeable about most of them. What he did not know Carl did. Rick knew after today that he had made new friends with Carl and Joyce. They were lovely people, after all.

Over dessert, Carl turned to Rick and said, "If it is ok with Mary and Joyce, we have a small apartment above our garage that is not being used. Instead of you paying for a hotel next week, you are welcome to stay up there. Is that ok with you girls?"

Joyce said, "That would be wonderful."

Mary hesitated with a smile, "I guess that would be ok."

"Good, that is settled. Now, this boy needs to get going back to the Army."

"Yes, I do, it is a long haul, and 0600-hours comes pretty darn early."

Mary walked Rick to his Jeep, grabbing his hand when they got a safe distance from the house.

"I don't know what you did there, soldier boy, but you sure turned my dad around in your direction."

"I don't know what I did either. I wasn't really trying very hard."

Rick pulled Mary close and said, "Let's not worry about how, just that we did something right, and I get to see you again next weekend. Pretty nice, huh."

"Yes, it is," Mary stood on her toes and gave Rick a kiss.

It was nice, warm, and sweet.

"Something to get you through the week, my dear."

"I appreciate that," said Rick.

"Why don't you bring your snorkel gear next weekend? I have a place I would like to show you."

"That would be nice. I never turn down a good dunk in the water, you know."

Rick got in the Jeep and waved goodbye to Mary in the rearview mirror.

Off for the long drive to Augusta.

CHAPTER 5
VW Fix

It was an easy week for Rick playing Army. He played his short-timer card a lot. The usual leading of the 0600-hours PT session was never fun, but it did get him going in the morning. He drove the Colonel around a few times, which is always easy duty except for the having to look sharp and kiss a lot of officer ass. Even the long and tedious stockade guard duty seemed to go without any problems. Word must have gotten out about the last weeks shotgun blast, as no prisoners even came close to his guard tower. In fact, they all stayed on the opposite side of the yard during his entire duty time. The long hours in the guard tower were always brutal but well worth it to get Fridays off.

Rick was finding that guard duty and the long drive to Lake City were both excellent times to think. On this guard duty he found himself mainly thinking about Mary. Pleasant thoughts but concerning thoughts. In a very short time, he was going to have his long-awaited freedom. After three long years of being told what to do every waking hour, he would be able to control his own actions and destiny. He was looking forward to only him controlling his every move. This meant that he did not want to get tied down to anything or anyone. Not being able to get Mary out of his mind was becoming a concern. He needed to keep living for the moment and not think about going forward with any plans for his life or with anyone else's life. He needed to be very careful about getting too attached to anything or anyone that would interfere with this goal.

After Friday morning's PT session, Rick got on the road to Lake City before 0800 hours. He had stopped by Ed and Monika's the night before and picked up his tools and diving gear, so he was able to head out of town right away. It was a beautiful early summer's morning. Driving south was nice, as the morning sun was off to his left and not blinding him. The drive to Lake City was becoming effortless as he was getting used to the route and it was not much different than heading to the corner grocery store. He did love the open road, and the southern scenery was lovely, especially early in the morning. And the thinking time was always welcome.

He arrived in Lake City a little past noon and drove straight to Mary's house. He knew that Mary and her dad were working but Mary's mother was supposed to be home. She must have heard him drive up, as she was already out the door of the screened-in porch before he got out of his Jeep. Rick met her halfway between his Jeep and the house. She was drying her hands on a dishtowel as she approached him.

"Well, hello Rick, it is nice to see you. So glad you could make it down here again."

While still holding the dishtowel in one hand, she put her arms around Rick and gave him a big hug. Rick's family had not been very affectionate people and hugs and kisses did not exist. Even verbal signs of endearment were rare. Probably why Mary's mother's hugs and affection made him a little uncomfortable, especially since he barely knew her.

"How are you doing, ma'am?" That was all Rick could think to say, and he knew it sounded a little shaky.

Mary's mother sensed his awkwardness, released her hug, and said, "Mary and Carl are both working and should be home around six. Can I get you anything?"

"No, thank you, I am fine. I was hoping to get started working on Mary's car, so I could maybe finish it before she got home."

"Of course," she said. "Why don't I show you the apartment first so you can get settled in, and then you can start playing with that old car."

"Sounds good."

Rick grabbed his old green Army duffle bag, something out of habit that he took everywhere with him. He followed Mary's mother to the garage. The garage was quite a distance from the house, maybe 100 feet or more. The pathway was white and packed with ground-up seashells. The garage itself was a cinder block building painted a bright white that matched the house. It had two large garage doors. On the far side, just past the last door and around the corner, was a long staircase that went up outside the building. At the top of the stairs was a large landing with a small table and two chairs. Rick paused at the top to look out at the view as Mary's mother unlocked the door. It was facing west and had a wide-open, panoramic view of the countryside. It overlooked a large pasture-like area that was spotted with small bodies of water. Trees and small bushes lined the fence rows on each side. Further out was a larger pond and then more trees. This was all backdropped by a cloudless blue sky.

"This is a lovely view from up here," Rick said.

"Yes, it is, probably one of the best around. Mary's mother said as she turned from the now unlocked door. "It is hard to find anything where you can see very far in Central Florida."

"It is pretty flat around here," answered Rick. "It's nice to see a wide-open area like this. I've noticed that all the vegetation in the South gives you a closed-in feeling."

Mary's mother turned and held the door open for Rick. "Here we are."

"Thank you," Rick answered back as he set his duffle bag down on the hardwood floor.

61

The room was small but very tidy and bright. A double bed was in one corner on the east wall, and a small couch was in front of an older model TV. Along another wall were a kitchen counter, stove, and a small refrigerator. A small table with two chairs were directly in front of the stove. The only other door was to the bathroom that was basic from what Rick could see. Toilet, sink, and one of those metal shower-stalls with a white curtain.

"This is very nice," Rick said.

"We used to rent it out, but it got to be too much trouble and decided it was not worth all the effort. I know it is small, but it has everything that anyone should need. Make yourself at home and holler if you need anything."

"Thank you, ma'am."

"You don't have to call me ma'am. That makes me sound like an old lady. Just call me Joyce."

"Ok, thank you, Joyce, ma'am."

Mary's mother, laughing, said. "Just Joyce is ok. I know that ma'am thing is a hard one not to do for you polite boys."

Mary's mother turned and started walking down the stairs. Rick ran after her and asked. "Is it ok if I bring the VW up here on the concrete by the garage?"

"Of course, dear, the keys are in it."

"Thanks."

Rick walked around the back of the house where the VW was parked. It looked like it had been sitting in the same spot for a very long time. It had been mowed around, and it was surrounded by long, thick weeds. It finally started after over a dozen cranks and then barely. It was running so rough that Rick had to pump the gas continually to keep it running. He finally got it running well enough to drive it out of the backyard and up to the garage area. It stalled as soon as he took his foot off the accelerator.

"This poor car has had a hard life for only 50,000 miles on it," Rick mumbled under his breath.

Rick pulled up the emergency brake, started the engine again, and let out the clutch slowly to test the clutch. If the clutch was ok, the car would stall or at least lunge forward. The emergency brake barely held but long enough to show that the clutch was slipping.

He pulled out the oil dipstick to look at its condition. Even though it was like molasses, it did not smell burnt, so things in the engine were probably ok.

"I am so sorry, you poor thing," Rick mumbled gently into the engine compartment.

Rick thought *This is going to be a little more of a job than I realized.*

He got out his notebook and started writing down possible problems and parts that he was going to need:

Plugs and points

Adjust timing

Adjust valves

Valve cover gaskets

Adjust clutch (hopefully just an adjustment)

Check brakes

Emergency brake (hopefully just an adjustment)

Change oil

Adjust carburetor

Air filter oil change

"Ok, auto parts store, here we come," Rick mumbled. He then spoke back again at the engine compartment, "You hang in there, little fella, we are going to fix you up like new."

After giving a little pat on the VW's hood, Rick jumped in the Jeep and headed back into town.

The first thing Rick did with the VW was to pull out the old spark plugs. Spark plugs gave a good indication of what was happening with the engine. As he suspected, the electrodes were worn down to almost nothing. They were also worn at different levels, so the gaps were all different, which helped explain the uneven firing of the pistons. He re-gapped the new plugs and set them aside for later. Next, he removed the distributor cap and rotor. The electrodes were worn down on the cap, and the rotor electrode was almost gone and blackened. He pulled out the points, and they had deteriorated as badly as everything else. *Not a lot of spark was going anywhere. No wonder this thing was not running,* Rick thought. Rick lubed and installed the new points into the distributor. He adjusted the point gap, installed the new rotor, and snapped on the new distributor cap. Locking in the four spark plug wires and the coil wire, he spoke to himself in a quiet tone, "At least the spark plug wires are still in good shape."

VWs were notorious for their valve gaps that did not stay adjusted well. Before any tuning was to be done, he had to adjust the valves on each cylinder. He hated doing this as he had to crawl underneath the car and take off the valve covers. Then while under the car, the engine had to be turned over by hand by pulling on the generator v-belt. Only then could the proper valve clearance be adjusted. Rick purposely kept the plugs out so hand turning the engine would be easier. He adjusted the valve gap on one cylinder and then went on to the next. They then had to be rechecked and re-adjusted many times. The important thing was that they all had the same gap. It was time-consuming and not enjoyable. With only four cylinders on a VW, all the engine adjustments were critical as a small amount off on any of them, and the engine would not run well. After Rick was satisfied with all the adjustments, he installed new, well lubed, valve cover gaskets, and snapped the valve covers back into place. He installed the new spark plugs and connected the plug wires, coupling each wire with the correct cylinder. Rick had made that mistake before. Only once, as the engine will not run well at all if they are wrong. He connected his timing light, loosened the distributor lock bolt, and put a chalk mark on the flywheel pulley. Rick started the engine. It sounded better already. He twisted the distributor till he got the exact timing and clamped it down. He pulled off the air filter so the carburetor could get good unrestricted airflow. Rick always hated these VW air filters as the air was filtered through an oil bath instead of a paper element. They were messy, and most people never check the oil quality in them. This one was an excellent example of that. The oil in the filter had a significant film over the top, and the oil was black as coal with dirt. It needed to be drained and replaced if the engine was going to get any oxygen. Rick started the tedious job of adjusting the air/fuel mixture on the carburetor with the air filter off. This was the final step to get the engine running smoothly. He adjusted the carburetor as well as he could. It was all by sound and there were a lot of variables. He drained, cleaned, and put new oil in the air filter. He started the engine and feathered the carburetor linkage, forcing gas into the cylinders. The engine roared up and settled back down instantly. He repeatedly opened the throttle many times, and each time it settled back down with a solid, crisp sound.

"Damn, you are good, Ricky boy," he said out loud with a hint of pride.

Rick left the engine running and went into the house and ask Mary's mom for a flat pan to drain the oil into. She followed him back out to the garage and came out with an old laundry basin.

"Will this work?" she said.

"That will be perfect, thank you."

"No thank you, for doing all this work on Mary's car. It would certainly not have gotten done around here. Carl is picking up Mary at the diner around six, so we should eat around seven if that is, ok?"

"That sounds good," said Rick. A slight flare of excitement hit him just by the sound of Mary's name.

Rick drained the oil and replaced it with some good racing oil that he always used. He pulled the tires and checked all the brakes.

Someone must have put new brakes on as they were all in excellent shape. The emergency brake was not holding. VW had made that an easy fix, as the adjustment was right above the emergency brake handle. With a few twists of two nuts at the cable end, the brake was grabbing like new. Rick re-tested the clutch by putting on the newly adjusted emergency brake, started the engine, put it in first gear, and slowly let out the clutch pedal. The clutch was for sure slipping. VW had made life simple again by controlling the clutch with a cable. The adjustment for the clutch was on the clutch cable that was back by the transmission. The transmission was in front of the engine, so Rick had to crawl deep under the car. At the side of the transmission was a wing nut on the clutch cable. The cable was extremely loose, so he knew that the tension was the problem. After adjusting it to the correct tension, he did the same clutch test. The car lunged forward and almost stalled. The clutch was grabbing perfectly.

"Well, that should do it," Rick said out loud.

He took it out for a test drive. Rick was pleased with himself as the old VW ran like it was new. Back at the garage, Rick found a bucket and hose. He cleaned and detailed the old car inside and out. He had bought some degreaser at the auto store, so he cleaned all the old dirt and oil off the engine. The whole car looked like it just came off the showroom floor. Rick had always been good at making old vehicles shine. Admiring his masterpiece, he thought, *what I must do to impress my dates.* He smiled with a personal sense of pride.

Rick cleaned up his car repair mess and took a long shower in his new apartment. The shower was definitely needed. His leading PT that morning, the long trip, and the day's work on the VW all affected his aroma. The water had the typical Florida strong sulfur smell, but Rick did not mind as the shower was so welcomed. After his shower, the bed was calling his name. He stretched out on the bed to rest his eyes for a few moments but ended up taking a long afternoon nap. He fell asleep still smiling at his VW accomplishment.

"Knock, knock," came a voice from the door at the top of the stairs. "Is anybody home?"

Rick did not have time to answer in his groggy state. The door flew open, and in came a pink blur, rushing across the room towards his bed.

"The car looks just wonderful, Mr. Rick."

Rick was lying on his back, and before he could get up, Mary had pulled her waitress uniform skirt up enough so she could jump onto the bed. With one continuous motion, she threw her left leg over the top of Rick. She was straddling Rick like she was riding a horse. Rick was both a little shocked but very much excited.

Mary's beauty was indeed a pleasant sight to wake up to, especially when she was on top of him.

Rick was still speechless, so Mary was the first to speak, "If that old car runs as good as it looks, we will be ready for Daytona."

She lowered her body down farther on top of Rick's and gave him a quick kiss on the lips. She then jumped off him as fast as she had jumped on. Rick knew it was Mary just being Mary, with all her energy and innocence. The feel of her body on his, however, had given him a rush of heat and excitement.

Mary stood beside the bed and yanked on Rick's hand, trying to pull him out of bed.

"Come on, lazy bones, my mother has her famous meatloaf on the table, and she doesn't like to serve cold food."

"Ok, but I need a minute to wake up here and get these cobwebs out of my head."

What Rick really needed to do was sit on the side of the bed for a few minutes until his excitement went away. Rick slowly stood up from the bed, put on his shoes, and walked over to the mirror for a quick look. Before he could tidy up his hair, Mary grabbed his hand, led him out the door, down the stairs, and into the house.

Briefly stopping at the front door, Mary squeezed Rick's hand and gave him a friendly kiss on the cheek.

"Are you ready for this," she said.

"After fighting with an old VW all afternoon, I can handle anything, my dear."

The supper was a great event, as Mary's mother was an excellent cook. They all made Rick feel very much at home and comfortable. Who would have thought, from the cold reception Rick got just a week ago. Carl had endless questions for Rick as to what all he did to the VW. Rick thoroughly enjoyed explaining everything to him.

At the end of supper, Rick looked directly at Mary and said, in a louder tone, so everyone could hear, "Why don't you and your dad take the car out for a test drive and see how it runs. I will help your mother clean up."

"No, you do not have to help me, Rick."

"Oh, but I insist, and I am anxious to see if the VW passes the inspection."

When Mary and her dad returned from their test drive, Carl could not say enough how well the car ran and how amazed he was. He noted his appreciation many times and said, "It is like a new car."

Rick was looking at Mary out of the corner of his eye and could see that she was happily smiling.

"Ok," Mary jumped up and interrupted, "Rick has had a very long day and needs his rest, as I have a surprise adventure for him tomorrow." She glanced over at her dad and smiled.

"Thank you so much for the nice supper, Joyce."

"And thanks again for everything you did on Mary's car."

"Yes, son, we do appreciate it," added Carl.

Mary walked Rick out of the house, and as soon as they hit the outside air, Mary grabbed Rick's hand and did not let go until they got to the garage stairs. At the top of the stairs, Rick took Mary's other hand and turned her towards him.

"Now, what is this big surprise thing for tomorrow?"

"You'll see. You will need your bathing suit, snorkel gear, and your Jeep, of course."

"Ok," is all Rick said. "What time?" he added.

"Oh, I will come and wake you up, mister."

"I am in the Army, remember, and have gotten up at 0600-hours for three years now. I doubt if you will beat me up."

"Don't count on that buddy, I am up with the chickens."

"We will see about that," said Rick. "I am out running about six."

Still holding hands, Rick pulled Mary close, and they exchanged another kiss. This time it was not a short kiss. It was a long kiss. It was a softer kiss. The longest and softest yet. This time a spark of passion kindled within both, something that had not happened before.

Afterward, they both paused and just looked at each other.

"Sleep well," said Rick.

"You too, and a very good night to you," Mary said as she turned and walked down the stairs. She did a slight wave at the bottom of the stairs and went to the house. Rick had a feeling that they both would be thinking of each other throughout the night. Rick certainly was going to be thinking of her.

CHAPTER 6
First Adventure

Rick was up as usual at 0600-hours. He sat up in the bed and looked out the east window at the sun rising, thinking about Mary and his love of the mornings. Rick knew why he loved sunrises, but it was still a mystery why this woman was bothering him. He also looked around the tiny apartment, thinking how great it was. It got the sunrise in the morning and the sunset at night. It was high above everything else in the area, so the view was amazing. He could see everything in all directions. He thought, *sort of like his guard tower,* then quickly thought, *no, it is not, you idiot, not even close.*

At that stupid thought, he quickly jumped out of bed and put on his running shorts, running shoes, and old Army T-shirt.

Opening the door, he stepped out onto the landing and into the crisp Florida air. It was so nice.

"About time you rolled out of bed, you lazy bum."

At the bottom of the stairs was Mary leaning against the stair rail.

She had on white shorts, running shoes, and a red tank top. Her long hair was tied back in a ponytail out of the way of her big, beautiful smile. She had wrapped her hair in a blue headband.

"Did you think you were the only one around here that could get up early and go for a little run?"

"A," Rick was speechless as he walked down the stairs towards her.

Before Rick could say anything, Mary said, "Hope you don't mind if I join you."

"Not at all," Rick managed a few words.

"Good morning, Mr. Rick," Mary said as she reached up and put her arms around his neck and gave him a sweet kiss on the lips.

"You are looking very patriotic this morning," Rick said, "Did you plan it that way?"

"No, I didn't plan it that way, but I guess it will make you feel like you are back at Fort Gordon."

"Please," Rick said, "If I had fellow soldiers looking the way you do, I would re-enlist tomorrow."

Ignoring Rick's comment, Mary said, "Let's go, soldier boy." She then turned and started running up her driveway.

"I have a little trail through the swamp that I like to run on," she shouted over her shoulder.

Still not moving, Rick was staring at Mary running off in those lovely white shorts and got him a little excited again until he snapped out of it.

"Crap, she is fast, and I am still standing here in shock," he mumbled to himself.

"Wait up," he yelled.

"Not on your life, soldier boy," Mary yelled as she kept running.

Rick finally caught up to Mary on the main road, only because she slowed down.

Running side by side, Rick said with an out-of-breath wheeze, "I am surprised that you're a runner and an early riser."

"I have a lot of surprises that you do not know about, mister."

"I am starting to believe you do, girl."

Mary quickly, without warning, turned off the road and headed down a small path. The path was so narrow that they had to run in a single file. As runners, they both knew that there would not be much conversation between running single-file and the lack of oxygen.

"Me leading does not infringe on your manhood, does it, my dear?" Mary yelled back.

"Not at all, my sweet; in fact, I am enjoying the view in front of me."

"You are so bad."

The trail was very narrow, maybe 3 feet wide, with waist-high vegetation on each side. The growth was so thick that you could not see past the green. The trail itself was white sand packed down from heavy use. An occasional stretch of deep sand would challenge the ankle and calf muscles running through it. Mary, of course, did not slow down. There was also an occasional vine root that stretched across the trail that had to be hopped over. There would often be an opening in the dense vegetation, and higher trees would always follow a small water pond. The trees did an eerie strobe light effect as they ran, and the morning sun shined through them.

After about a mile or two, Mary stopped in front of Rick. She bent over and put her hands on her knees, with her face looking at the ground, breathing very heavily. Rick did the same thing with an equal number of breaths. He did manage to keep one inconspicuous eye at Mary's white shorts and what was in them. *You are such a dirty old man,* Rick thought to himself. *She is such a pleasant vision, though.*

"Ok, Ricky boy," Mary stood upright and faced him with her hands on her hips, "Are you ready for the home stretch?"

"Yes, Drill Sergeant," Rick said as he stood up also and gave Mary a sloppy salute.

Mary ran off with Rick following close behind.

Rick always had to lead the PT runs in the Army, so it was pleasant just to follow and enjoy the morning sunshine and the run.

They got back to the bottom of Rick's stairs, where they both had to catch their breaths for a few minutes.

"How about you come into the house for a little breakfast," Mary said. "My dad had to go into work for a little while, but my mother is home, and you know she can make a mean breakfast."

"Sounds great," said Rick.

"Then you need to shower up, get into your swimsuit, and get your diving stuff together." We are going on that adventure I promised."

"I bet you are still not going to tell me what or where we are going, are you?"

"Nope. For me to know and you to find out."

"That is pretty corny, you know."

"Yup."

"Ok, I will trust you."

"You better, mister."

"Oh, and bring tennis shoes instead of your sandals."

After breakfast and a quick shower, Rick met Mary at his Jeep. Rick had his mask, fins, snorkel, and a towel as instructed. Mary came out of the garage struggling, carrying a huge duffle bag.

"Glad you travel light with your diving gear, girl," Rick said with a smirk and lifting his gear in the air with one hand.

"This is part of your surprise, silly."

Rick's gear was all in a backpack, so he quickly tossed them in the back of the Jeep. The rear tailgate on the Jeep was nice, as you could lower it, making loading easy. Rick met her and grabbed the duffle with one hand and, with a single motion, tossed it into the back of the Jeep.

Mary went back and got her backpack and threw it in the back of the Jeep, and they were off, heading south on highway 47. After around thirty minutes, they turned onto a secondary road, then onto a very rough trail road that obviously had little use. There were a lot of deep ruts and washed-out gullies. The Jeep had a tight suspension, so Rick and Mary bounced around a lot. Thick forest and scrub bushes were all along the road, and as in most of Florida, you did not see a great distance in any direction. They came to an opening with a wide-open area that looked like a crude parking area.

"Here we are," said Mary.

"And just where is, here?" said Rick.

"You will see."

Rick started to park the Jeep, but Mary jumped out before he came to a stop. She jumped into the back of the Jeep and started to haul the duffle bag out.

"Here, let me get that, Wonder Woman."

Before he could get the tailgate down, Mary had already tossed it to the ground like a dock worker, where it landed with a thump. She bent over and opened the end of the duffle.

"You grab the back of the bag, Ricky boy, and I will pull this beast out of here at this end."

Rick pulled, and Mary pulled until the contents broke loose suddenly, sending Mary flying backward onto her backside in the sand.

"That was fun," she said with a note of sarcasm. She sat on her backside with her knees spread in front of her. In between her legs was this giant, gray, rubber blob.

"Where is a camera when you need one," Rick said as he reached his hand out to help Mary up.

"And this would be?" Rick said with a long, drawn-out tone.

"You know what it is," Mary stated with an, of course, you know voice, "This is the old rubber raft that I have had since High School."

"That's old," Rick said. "Does it float?"

"Of course, it does. It has been on some great adventures. I call it my little Puffy."

Mary unfolded Puffy, pulled out a foot pump, and started blowing it up.

Puffy was inflated in less than five minutes.

It was a small raft with a gray color on the outside and a dark blue interior. There were two paddles, each in two pieces. There was a handle in front and one in back, the front had a long rope tied to it. It was basic but had plenty of room for two people and gear.

"This is my simple little raft." Mary said. "It's small and doesn't look like much, but it is a rugged one. It has a sharkskin fabric that can take about anything, and it won't puncture. I have dragged it over coral before, and it didn't even get a scratch."

"It is pretty cool," Rick said. "I like it."

"I thought you would."

"We have a little hike to get to where we are going. Why I told you to bring tennis shoes instead of sandals, the Sandspurs can be wicked on bare feet."

They both had their bathing suits on. Rick had his regular old boxer type and Mary had a lovely two-piece. Rick was covered with a t-shirt while Mary had a white cotton sundress. It was very sheer and was almost a see-through so the outline of her two-piece bikini underneath was showing through. They both had their backpacks with a towel and diving gear. Rick brought a couple of beers, and Mary had packed a lunch.

"Ok, Mister, let's get moving," Mary said as she placed her backpack over both her shoulders. Of course, Rick noticed how the pressure of the backpack straps amplified the shapeliness of Mary's front side.

Get a grip, Rick thought as he found himself getting a little excited again. The moment was short-lived, as Mary already tossed the paddles into the raft and had grabbed the front handle.

"Let's go, soldier, grab the stern handle and let's move. We are burning daylight."

"We are burning daylight?" Rick repeated and laughed. "You have been watching too many old John Wayne movies, haven't you?"

"Just get moving, pilgrim."

They both laughed as Rick grabbed the rear handle and lifted the raft.

God, I like this lady, Rick thought.

Mary took off so fast that Rick had to stumble to keep on his feet.

It was another narrow trail, not unlike the one they had run that morning. The vegetation was very thick on each side. The path was so thin that the raft continually rubbed and pushed aside the plants and bushes. The sand was not as hard as the morning run, so it was hard to walk in. It seemed like not many people hiked this area, as there would be an occasional scampering and slithering of critters escaping away from them. Rick was undoubtedly wondering where Mary was taking him. It was an exciting wonder.

After a quarter mile, they came to a wide opening in the vegetation where they stood on a large outcrop of limestone. They overlooked a blue-green body of water, that was as clear as a freshly drawn bath.

Mary and Rick let go of the raft handles simultaneously, and it dropped to the limestone with a muffled thump. They both took off their tennis shoes and backpacks. Mary grabbed Rick's hand and led him out into the water on the rock slab. At about ankle-deep, they stopped, still holding hands, and looked out over the water.

The limestone rock extended out into the water past where they were standing. There was one tiny little natural step, but the rest of it gradually submerged itself into the blue. The pond was surrounded by vegetation, except for an opening at the far end. This opening flowed into a river and then got lost between large overhanging trees. The water extended in front of them to the shore on the other side. It was not very far, maybe the width of a football field. To the left of the pond was a small beach, no larger than a pickup truck. Two prominent clumps of tall weeds floated in the water. Fallen trees divided the weeds directly in the middle. Trees appeared to grow out of the water at the river opening, with many branches touching the surface. The rest was just beautiful blue, green, aqua, colored water.

"This is amazing," Rick said as he squeezed Mary's hand a little tighter.

"I thought you would like it," said Mary as she squeezed his hand back.

"How in the heck did you know about this place?"

"Us locals know about many of these places, and we have tried to keep them a secret. We must keep those nasty tourists out of here, you know. My friends and I have been coming here and to other of our secret places for years. We partied here a lot and floated the river starting back in high school. We used to have to sneak in here as this whole area was privately owned. We got chased out now and then by security guards. Just recently, the State of Florida bought this whole area from this big mining company that owned it. Some phosphate company, I think. Rumor is they will turn all of it into a state park or something like that. Which is good, I guess, but bad for us locals and our little secret places. Not to mention the masses of people that will be coming in here. Right now, nobody comes here. I mean, look at this, we are it, our own little private swimming hole."

"Pretty cool," Rick said again, "I love it. So, madam tour guide, what's our plan?"

Still holding hands, Mary pulled Rick over to her.

"First of all, Ricky boy, you are going to give me a nice kiss."

Rick happily obeyed, and while still standing in the water, they shared a nice soft kiss.

Mary let go of Rick's hand and put her arm around his waist. Rick responded by putting his arm around her neck and shoulders.

"I thought we would first put on our diving gear and float around this spring for a little while. As you can see, it is amazing. Then we'll load up everything into Puffy and paddle her downriver. Then we're going to stop at another spring down the river and have a nice lunch. We'll do a little more diving there and then head a little farther downriver. How about that?"

"That sounds just wonderful, my dear. You're my kind of woman for sure. How far do we go downriver?"

"A couple of miles or more," said Mary.

Rick paused for a moment, obviously thinking.

Rick slowly said, "Now I see one little hiccup in your plan. I have noticed that the water moves out of here very fast, which means a strong current. And, no offense, but little Puffy here does not have the best aerodynamics on the block. Paddling back upstream a few miles could be nasty."

"I did not realize that you were such a wimp. I thought you were this big tough soldier."

Rick stuttered slightly, "Yes, but."

Before Rick finished, Mary laughed, "By the expression on your face, I could tell I had you a little worried there, didn't I? My dad's going to pick us up downstream this afternoon and bring us back to your Jeep, silly."

"You think you are so funny, don't you," Rick said as he swooped Mary up in his arms and carried her to the edge of the rock outcrop and dropped her into the clear water, cotton dress, and all. Mary screamed when she hit the cold water.

Rick held out his hand and helped her back up onto the rock.

Taking off her soaked dress and wringing it out, Mary said, "Oh, you will pay for that one, mister. Not now, but soon, and you won't know when it is coming."

"Oh, I'm scared," said Rick

"Well, you better be," Mary said as she pointed her finger at Rick, then walked closer and gave him a very long kiss.

They slipped their masks, with snorkels attached, on the top of their heads. With their swim fins in one hand and holding hands with the other, they walked down the limestone rock into the water. They started floating immediately around the pond.

The water was a chilly 70 degrees coming right out of the spring, but it felt great in the summer heat. As they got closer to the spring, the temperature of the water dropped drastically and the current increased. The water was so clear and clean. The sun projected and amplified the surface ripples onto the sandy bottom like wiggling glow worms.

Mary led Rick by his hand to the spring where the water was coming out. It was a large hole in the pond bottom, six feet in diameter, with a blue/black color at its center. Surrounding it was a circle of sand, and around the sand was a large field of tall water grass. The grass circled the spring, and it was dancing to the rhythm of the outflowing water. It was swaying back and forth with a steady motion to the beat of the underground aquifers as its precious fluid emptied into the river.

Mary and Rick did a surface dive down into the spring but could get only within a few feet as the current coming out was intense.

Rick was in awe of everything in the pond, especially Mary, and he did not tire of seeing any of it.

Rick and Mary had both been diving since they were very young. Rick in Michigan and Mary in Florida. They both were completely at home in the water, and they both loved it. This water-bond was eventually going to be the start of their falling in love. They finally left the water, being a little chilly and wrinkled. Putting their towels down on Puffy's floor, they settled down together on the sun-warmed rubber. It was a little cramped, so Rick lifted his arm and put it around Mary's neck as she moved over and put her head on his chest. They rested there for a long while, just looking up at the blue sky, and feeling the warm sun on their wet bodies.

"Not bad, girl, not bad," Rick said as he kissed Mary on the top of her head.

After enjoying the sun for a while, Mary finally said, "Ok, we need to get moving as we have a dad to catch later, and I want to spend some time at Blue Hole Spring for lunch."

"You are the boss, lady."

They packed all their gear into their backpacks and tossed them into the raft. Mary grabbed the front handle with a paddle in one hand, and Rick did the same with the back. They hauled Puffy into the water.

CHAPTER 7
Floating the River

Mary turned around and looked at Rick, "I guess I should have asked you if you have ever paddled anything before. Shouldn't I have?"

"Yes, you should have. We could be in serious trouble."

Rick paused then answered, "I am from Michigan, you know, I have been paddling, rowing, and floating things since I could walk."

"Great," Mary said, "then you can take the stern and do all the steering and the work."

"That's fine with me as I love to be in control."

They floated the raft and headed for the opening at the far end of the pond. The channel was small, and there were low branches from the trees hanging over the water where they had to drop down into Puffy to pass. Once on the open river, the current was strong enough so very little paddling was needed. The river was just as clear as the spring. The depth was probably six to ten feet, but it looked very shallow. Rick had not paddled for a while, but it all came back very quickly. Once learned as a child; the J-stroke, backstroke, and sidestroke were never forgotten.

"You've done this before, haven't you, Rick? You never stop amazing me."

"You never stop amazing me either, lady," Rick said as he watched Mary paddle the front of Puffy through some tall weeds. Her strong back muscles were bulging out around the small strap on her bikini.

Damn, this woman is sure exciting, Rick thought. *What is with that?*

The river started out relatively narrow, with trees and bushes almost touching the sides of the raft. A cypress tree had fallen entirely across the river and was partially submerged. The center part was sunken more than the rest of the tree, so there was enough water to pass over it. The bottom of Puffy, however did scrape all the way across. The tall water grasses that were almost reached the surface, were lying flat, indicating that the current was very fast. Just before Puffy left the narrow stream, a low-lying branch stretched across the water, forcing Mary and Rick onto the floor of the raft once again. When they floated out in the wider river, the current seemed not as strong, so Rick and Mary had a chance to relax and enjoy the nature. On a small island of floating big-leafed plants a large white bird with long legs watched Rick and Mary float by. It didn't move away or fly, just looked at the two boaters for a second and resumed feeding in the vegetation.

"Egret," Mary said. There are a lot of them along here. Pretty, aren't they?"

"Beautiful, Rick said, "Those long tiny feathers hanging down into the water are amazing, and it does not seem concerned with us being here."

"They don't see many humans along here," Mary said.

"Are there any alligators in here?" asked Rick.

"I have never seen one in all the times I have been coming here. I think the water might be a little too cold for them, especially up here close to the head spring."

The whole river was almost like a tunnel without a ceiling, as the trees were so tall all along both banks that nothing could be seen past the river's edge. Most of the trees were covered with Spanish moss hanging off their branches. Much of the time, the moss was touching the water surface. A large cypress tree had fallen halfway across the river and was hanging two feet off the water. Three turtles had climbed halfway out onto the log and were sunning themselves.

"Painted Turtles," Mary said.

They did not move as they paddled by.

The river was much wider now, almost like a lake.

The bottom of the river was covered with white sand at many points, and at other times the water plants completely covered it.

"How about snakes?" Rick asked.

"I have seen many of them, but they hang out in those weed patches along the shores. Seldom do we see them in the middle of the river."

"Not a big fan of snakes," Rick said, "especially the ones that kill you."

"You're a little wimp," said Mary.

With his paddle, Rick sent a plume of water at Mary, and it made a direct hit. Mary returned a larger splash that completely soaked Rick.

"Don't mess with me, buster."

"I can see that, so sorry," said Rick as he shook the water out of his hair.

They were both dripping wet now, but that condition does not last long in the hot Florida sun.

"Around the next bend, we're going to turn into another spring for lunch. How does that sound?" Mary said.

"Sounds like a good plan to me."

They turned off the main river and entered a lagoon-like area. Off to the right was a small sandy beach. This pond was not as big as the headwater spring but had taller trees and more water vegetation around the edges. In fact, there was a lot of floating vegetation all around the pond except where the small beach was. There was another lovely beach on the far side, but it had masses of floating vegetation in front of it. The bottom was mostly covered with tall water grasses instead of beautiful white sand like the other spring.

"That is where we'll stop, but I want to float over the spring first," Mary said.

The weed-covered bottom was a green-brown until it broke into a sandy circle area. In the center, down about 20 feet, was a giant black hole. It looked so out of place, like an underwater island.

"This is the spring," said Mary. "Us locals call it Blue Hole. It goes down there pretty deep."

"Love it," said Rick.

They beached Puffy, and Mary quickly started walking into the low-hanging brush.

"Excuse me, sir, but I must go check out the local plant life."

Rick knew well where she was going as he had a similar urge.

"Floating on all that water does it you know," yelled Rick.

Rick went off in the other direction.

Back at the raft, Mary said, "How about we go for a little snorkel out to the spring and then make some lunch."

"You're the tour guide, boss lady."

They got their diving gear on and walked on the weedy bottom out into the deeper water. The water grass was very thick and felt like a blanket on their bare feet. Small fish were darting in and out of the grass as it swayed with the current. When the water got waist deep, they put on their swim fins, lowered their masks, and started floating. They got over the top of the spring, and it looked like a big black hole in the ground, with the white sand surrounding it amplifying the darkness. They both did some surface dives to get down into the spring as far as possible, but the current was strong, and they had no weight belts.

Coming back to shore, they took their swim fins off in the deeper water. With fins in one hand and their free hand in each other's, they negotiated the tall water weeds again. They held each other's hand for stability but mostly because it was very nice.

Rick got the two beers out of his backpack back at the raft, and Mary started preparing a little lunch. Rick opened the beers and handed one to Mary.

"Here you go, lady, you earned this one."

"Thanks."

Mary set out some cheese and crackers and a large bag of fresh, cut-up tropical fruits.

They sat next to each other on the floor of Puffy, leaning on the rubber side tubes as backrests.

"How deep does that spring go?" Asked Rick.

"I have some local guy friends that have dived into it, and they said it goes pretty deep."

"Have you ever dived into a cave?" asked Rick.

"Oh no, that is not for me." snapped back Mary. "I dive about anywhere, but nowhere that I can't get to the surface. Have you ever cave dived?"

"When I went to school at Edison, down in Fort Myers, a couple of my diving buddies took me into some shallow caves. It was pretty interesting, a whole different world."

"No thanks," Mary said again.

"I wouldn't mind trying this one sometime," Rick said. "I bet Ted would be up for it. Do you remember Ted? He was one of the guys at the diner."

"Oh, that famous diner night. I don't remember Ted as I only had eyes for you that night, dear." Mary said in a sarcastic tone.

"You are so full of it," Rick said. "But I like what you are full of."

He leaned over and gave Mary a small kiss on the cheek.

While only backing their faces away a few inches, they looked at each other for a second and fell into a long and passionate kiss. It might have been more extended and more passionate, but Mary's foot kicked over one of the beers, and it flowed freely onto the bottom of the boat.

"Oops," Mary said as she scrambled to tip it back upright.

"We had better rinse that off before my dad picks us up. I do believe he still thinks I don't drink beer."

"We wouldn't want to change that image, would we?" said Rick.

"Speaking of my dad, we had better get going downriver. I don't want him to wait very long as he was very nice to pick us up. It was actually his idea, you know. I think he likes you."

"That's nice, but I hope his daughter likes me more."

"You're growing on her," Mary said as she stood up from the floor of the raft and gave Rick another kiss."

They stuffed their gear into their backpacks, rinsed the beer from Puffy's floor, and were out on the main river again. The river had widened considerably after Blue Hole Spring. Still, the water channel was narrower because of all the floating vegetation coming off each bank. There was a long stretch where the river divided, and a large island of vegetation separated the two channels. They took the larger of the two. They paddled around one river bend where the bank had been undercut so much that there were tiny caverns into the hillside. They were able to paddle into the caverns around twenty feet, where they could look up at the ceiling. It was interesting seeing all the roots hanging down from the big trees and smaller grasses. Many side channels extended back into the vegetation.

"There are so many springs back at the end of these smaller creeks," Mary said. "I've been into a lot of them, but I'm sure that there are many that no one knows of, except the local Seminole Indians, of course. The vegetation gets so dense in a lot of them."

"Have you been down this one," Rick said as he pointed his paddle off to the left.

"That one I have, I don't know what they call it. We can go in there if you want. It gets narrow and shallow this time of year, so we might not get all the way in. I remember last time I was in there, we had to hike most of the way in."

Without saying a word, Rick did a quick side stroke and headed into the opening. Mary was right. After a few hundred feet, it got very narrow with lots of overhanging trees and branches. Paddling against a slight current added to the difficulty in navigating. Then there were old tree stumps coming straight up out of the water in the middle of the stream. Puffy's bottom started rubbing on some of them.

"Maybe we should save this for another adventure when we don't have to meet my dad," suggested Mary.

"I think that might be an excellent plan," answered Rick as he struggled to turn the boat around.

Getting out was easier as the current was now pushing them out into the main river.

"Actually," Mary said. "Around this next bend in the river is our spot where my dad is going to be."

"Already," answered Rick.

There was a small sandy beach on the left that Mary told Rick to head for. They pulled Puffy out of the water and opened the valves. Packed everything up and carried everything out to a small dirt path that, halfway, looked like a road. Mary's dad showed up soon afterward. He had his old pickup, so it was easy tossing the equipment in the back. It was a long drive over some nasty back roads before they got to the highway and back to Rick's Jeep. Mary's dad took off right away, and Rick and Mary were not far behind him.

When they got back to Lake City, it was still early, late afternoon. Rick lifted Puffy's duffle bag out of the back of the Jeep.

"Where would you like your little friend here, Mary?"

"It goes in the garage. Follow me, Mr. muscles."

Rick followed Mary into the garage and back to a small room in the far corner.

"In here would be great, thanks."

Rick noticed a lot of SCUBA diving equipment on one wall. "Is this all yours?" Rick asked with puzzlement.

"Of course, it is silly. You didn't think it was my parents, did you."

"Well, I thought it might be."

"You are kidding me, aren't you? My parents are not very happy that I am a diver. They would never think of doing such a thing."

"I thought you were just kidding about diving. How long have you dived?"

"I got certified way back in high school, I don't know, maybe I was seventeen."

"Your equipment looks pretty nice. How often do you go under?"

"I have not been out lately as all my dive friends have either gotten married or moved away. I did a trip to the Keys about six months ago with a couple of friends home from college."

"I am pleasantly impressed. I have not met many lady divers. That is very cool."

"How long have you been diving?"

"I got certified in 1962. Back when there were not a lot of divers around in Michigan. YMCA course for $12. I still carry my card around, and I still can get air with it."

Rick got out his wallet and showed Mary the old beat-up card.

"I got certified at our local dive shop, but it was a lot more than $12."

"The YMCA hired a couple of retired Navy Seals that enjoyed inflicting pain on us more than they should have. It was a brutal course, and they actually failed people. I have stories."

"Ours was pretty easy, and no one failed."

"We need to go diving sometime. What do you think?"

"I would love to get underwater again," answered Mary. "It's a long haul to the Keys, and I have so much to do getting ready for college this fall. Plus, I'm trying to work as much as I can to save up some money."

Rick paused and thought for a moment.

"You know what I was thinking while we were floating the river today? Have you ever tried floating it underwater?"

"No," Mary answered back slowly. "I have never known anybody who has done it."

"We could put on full SCUBA gear but snorkel a lot of the time and go under when we had the urge. That way, we would have plenty of air for the whole trip. As amazing as it was floating today in Puffy, can you imagine if we did it all underwater? The things we could see."

Mary was still thinking, but a spark of excitement started flickering.

"That would be pretty cool," she said. "We could actually go a lot farther than we did today. I know of some great coves that I would love to explore underwater. We would need a drop-off and pick-up vehicle."

"I bet Ed and Monika would love to come down and help us out. Ed is the one with the van on that famous diner night, remember?"

"I barely remember you that night, let alone Ed, Ted, or a van. I was just kidding about you, dear."

"You better be," Rick said as he tickled Mary in the ribs.

Mary retaliated with a series of finger jabs into Rick's ribs.

"Ok, sorry I started that," Rick said as he grabbed Mary's hand and pulled her in close and gave her a kiss on her lips. It got quiet for a minute in the garage as it ended up not being a short kiss.

"I wonder if my parents would be ok with a little overnight camping trip on the river?" Mary said as she quickly pulled back from Rick's embrace. "I know of a great beach downstream that is a great place to camp. I have not been camping for a long time. It would be so nice to sleep outside again, especially on the river."

"That would be pretty nice," Rick said. "A diver and a camper, how did I get so lucky. Now, if you only could cook and do laundry."

Rick got another series of finger pokes in his ribs.

"Is that a plan?" Rick said.

"I would love it," said Mary.

"I will check with my duty schedule and with Ed and Monika. I know they would be so happy with the camping thing as they don't dive, and it would give them something to do."

"I will work on my parents. They will not be happy with my diving and camping with a wild and crazy soldier boy. Wish me luck on that one."

"Good luck on that one," answered Rick

"Ok," Mary said. "Why don't you go up and take a shower and get ready for supper, and I will do the same. How about you come inside in about an hour."

"Yes, drill sergeant."

"I tried for that to not sound like an order, sorry."

"And I was just kidding."

Mary reached up and put her arms around Rick's neck and gave him a friendly kiss.

"Black tie is optional tonight, but if you want to impress my parents you should put on a tie," Mary said as she patted Rick on his chest where a tie should go.

"You are so funny," Rick said.

Rick was really starting to enjoy these meals with Mary and her parents. They talked and laughed a lot about silly little things. Everyone asked how everyone else was doing or feeling. They ate in peace with no yelling or complaining. Something that Rick had never got to experience with his family growing up. Everything in his family was always so serious around the household. Someone was constantly arguing or mad about something. This was so nice and how it should be. He never would have thought things would be like this after his first meeting, especially with Carl. He had turned out to be the most sociable and considerate man. He had really started to like Rick, even with him stealing his daughter from him.

"This is wonderful, blackened fish, Joyce," said Rick.

"Glad you like it. It is an old family recipe from my Cajun side of the family."

"What is the fish?"

"It is just an old piece of Cod, but the Cajun spices bring out the flavor in anything."

Rick looked over at Mary, and she was looking at him and smiling. Rick could tell that she was very happy that he was fitting in with her family so well.

"We didn't have much time to talk on the shuttle, so tell me, did you like the river float?" Mary's father asked.

"Don't get me started," said Rick, "It was just amazing. I couldn't get enough of it. I am so grateful to Mary for sharing it with me."

"I figured you would like it being the outdoor guy you are. I just hope the state does not wreck it by bringing in hordes of people."

There was a brief pause in the conversation.

"I hear you two are thinking of diving the whole river." Mary's father said with a half mouthful of cod.

"Where did you hear a silly thing like that?" Rick said as he glanced over at Mary, who was just smiling. "Was it Walter Cronkite on the evening news?"

"I think that is where I heard it," Mary's father said. "Or was it the sports section of the newspaper? One of those two." He did a slight chuckle.

"Someone does not waste any time getting news out around here, do they," Rick said.

"That could be a fun way to see the river," Mary's father said. "And pretty safe as long as you stay out of those big holes. I hear you have friends that can drop you off and pick you up?"

"Yes, Ed and Monika, I have known them for a long time. I knew them before I got orders for Nam. They are a married couple that live on base."

"When were you thinking of going?"

"I hadn't thought that far ahead yet, I guess. I'll have to see what my duty schedule is."

"That all sounds good to me. What do you think, Joyce?"

"As long as they're careful," she said. "You know I never have liked that underwater stuff."

"My mother hated my diving when I started also." said Rick. "She still is not really excited about it. She tells me not to tell her when I am going. I have been doing it since I was 15, and I am very careful."

"You are big kids now, so I would think you two will be ok. We still need to talk about the overnight camping thing, however," Mary's mother added.

"Walter Cronkite did not leave anything out in his report, did he," Rick said with a nervous laugh. This was followed by a second nervous laugh from the table. Then there was a pause in the conversation.

Mary's mother broke the pause; "Oh, I almost forgot, Linda called today and asked if Rick was going to be visiting and wanted to talk with you."

"What about?" asked Rick.

"Seems the band is going to be playing in Atlanta in a few weeks, and she wondered if you wanted to drive over from August and join them again."

"That was a lot of fun but again, it depends on my duty schedule."

"She is staying at the Hyatt Regency Hotel in the Peachtree Gardens area, as that is where they are playing. Have you been there?"

"Yes, I have. It is a pretty fancy place."

"She also invited all of us to join her. Carl and I have plans around here that weekend that we cannot get out of, so we can't go. That is too bad, as we would love to get up to Atlanta again. It has been a while. Can't remember the last time we were there. When was it, Carl?"

"Oh, it's been years. It's a long haul to get there."

"I bet it is closer than Augusta from here," Rick said.

"Might be, but you are young."

"It is only about two hours from Augusta," Rick said. "Have you ever been there, Mary?"

"We all went through there when I was pretty small on our way to the Smoky Mountains, but I don't remember much."

"When I told Linda that we could not make it, she asked if Mary would like to ride up with her as she was driving by herself."

Rick could see Mary trying to not show her excitement about the idea, but her eyes were giving her away.

"Would you be interested in going up there, honey?"

"It would be fun to see Atlanta," Mary said, trying to not act too excited.

"Linda said to let her know, and she would book a double room."

"That would be great," Mary said. "Plus, it will be a good test run for when I have to drive up to Chicago."

There was an uncomfortable silence around the table. Mary's parents were sad that she was going so far away from home to school.

"I will call Linda later tonight and let her know. I know she will be excited to hear you are going. I hope you can make it over there, Rick."

"Me too. It is hard to say. Things are getting a lot easier with duty as all the higher-ups realize I am a short-timer, and they know my attitude is not what it used to be."

"I do remember that" Mary's father added. "That was such a wonderful feeling knowing I was almost out of the Army."

"I do hear you," answered Rick.

They bonded.

Mary showed a subtle smile again for many reasons.

After supper, Mary and Rick helped her mother with dishes, Rick dried, and Mary put them away. Her mother always seemed to appreciate the help. Her father was old school, so he stayed sitting at the table reading the paper.

Mary was still smiling.

"It's almost eight. Is it ok if Rick and I go to the apartment and watch TV? *The Mary Tyler Show* is on, and I just know Rick would love to watch it with me."

"Oh, would I ever," Rick sarcastically answered.

Mary's father was listening to the conversation and just said, "Sorry, I cannot help you with that one, son." And laughed. "Or maybe I can," He picked up a TV Guide and, with his finger, traveled down the page. "Why look right here *Mission Impossible* is on right afterward."

"Oh great," Mary said.

"Thank you, sir," said Rick. "I owe you one."

The screen door had barely shut behind them when Mary grabbed Rick's arm and placed her head on Rick's shoulder as they walked to the apartment.

"I'm pretty happy right now," Mary said. "We can feasibly have at least two more nice weekends together."

"Hopefully, at least," Rick answered back.

He turned her towards him at the bottom of his stairs, and they shared a long kiss in the warm Florida darkness.

It was a small TV, but at least it was in color. Mary turned it on and turned it to *The Mary Tyler Moore Show* station while Rick went to the fridge.

"Would you like a beer, Mary?"

"Sounds good."

They cuddled on the small couch and shared kisses during the commercials. It was very nice.

Mission Impossible ended.

"I had better get back to the house. I know my parents will be waiting up."

Rick walked Mary to the bottom of the stairs, where they shared another long kiss good night. The kisses were getting more extended and more passionate as their relationship grew. They both found that it was getting harder to say the goodnights, let alone those goodbyes at the end of the weekend. They both were starting to think often about that inevitable final goodbye that was coming at the end of the summer.

"Are you up for another run in the morning, Mister?"

"If you are."

"Same time, soldier boy?"

"I can make it if you can."

"We'll see about that."

They did one last goodnight kiss.

"Hope you can outrun those mosquitos that are waiting out there for you."

"You know I am fast enough after kicking your butt this morning."

"We'll see tomorrow. Good night."

"Night."

Mary ran for the house as Rick watched.

"Damn," Rick said out loud and smiled.

The following morning Mary was at Rick's door at precisely six, but Rick was there to greet her this time. They did the same running route as the day before, but Rick enjoyed everything more this time. The mornings in Florida were so lovely before the sun gets high. The air is crisp but not cold. The moist air amplifies all the beautiful smells that have been waiting all night to come out. The birds are all so happy, and they let you know it with so many different notes. Maybe the best part of the day.

Back at Rick's apartment, he took a shower, stripped the sheets off the bed, cleaned the kitchen and bathroom, and packed up his gear in his duffle. He wanted to get an early start so he could get back on post at a decent hour. He wanted to get over to Ed and Monika's and see what they thought about a little trip to Florida. He knew they would be up for it as they'd always been up for a good adventure, and both had been getting bored on base. Also, Monika had been very curious about this new gal that Rick had been traveling to see.

Rick tossed all his gear into the back of his Jeep and walked to the house. Mary was in the kitchen cooking breakfast when Rick came in the door.

"Hope you are hungry as I am making you my uncle's famous biscuit-and-gravy recipe."

"I do love biscuits and gravy. My favorite breakfast, actually."

"Well, these will be the best you have ever had."

"Where are your parents?"

"Oh, they went to early church this morning, so it is just you and me, kid. They go out for breakfast after church on Sundays, so we have some alone time."

"Nice," is all Rick said. "I want to take off early so I can go over and visit Ed and Monika and ask them what they think about joining us on our river adventure. Plus, I need to drop off all my tools and diving gear before I go back to the barracks."

After a short silence, Mary said, "You do know that it's getting harder for me to see you go, don't you?"

"I was just thinking the same thing as I was packing this morning."

Rick walked over to Mary, who was at the stove, grabbed her around the waist, and kissed her neck. He stepped back.

"Can I help you with anything?"

"Why don't you pour us a cup of coffee."

They ate breakfast out on the porch sitting next to each other on some white wicker chairs and table. Mary was right, they were the best biscuits-and-gravy he had ever eaten.

"Did you hear from your parents about the camping trip thing?" Rick asked.

"We actually talked about it this morning before they left for church."

"And?"

"They said it was fine with them."

"Great."

"There was a lot of talk about being-good, if you know what I mean. Especially from my mother."

"Oh."

"Yes, it was a little uncomfortable."

"Better you than me."

"My father said he would have a little talk with you about things."

"Oh, wonderful," Rick said with an eye roll.

"I doubt if he will, so I wouldn't worry about it. I did tell them that I was 22 years old and that I have been around the block a few times."

"Bet they didn't care for that too much."

"No, they didn't, but they have always been pretty supportive and civil with me."

"It sure does look like you have a wonderful relationship with them."

"Yes, I do."

"I would have given anything to have had this warm a family."

"They are good, but they have just seen so many of my friends get into trouble at a young age and mess up their lives. These small towns, you know. Plus, they know how much I want to succeed in school. They only have my interests at heart."

"I can see that."

"So, we are good to go?"

"Yes, we are. It will be a fun adventure for sure."

"I did have to make a big promise to my mother, however, that I would be a good girl, and I need to keep it."

"Yes, you do," said Rick. "Plus, you know we are just good friends anyway, right."

Rick leaned over and gave Mary a friendly kiss on the cheek.

After an excellent long breakfast and a long talk on the porch, Mary walked Rick to his Jeep.

"Can you give me a call at home here when you find out things," Mary said.

"I will. I've been saving up my quarters for the payphone. Thank you so much for a lovely weekend," Rick continued. "It was truly amazing on the river with you."

"No, thank you for making my VW like new again and sharing the weekend with me." After a slight pause, Mary continued, "This was the best weekend I have had in quite a while where I could be myself and laugh as much as we have. It feels so natural and comfortable when we are together. Ok, enough of that, you need to hit the road."

"Thank you for saying exactly what I was thinking, I'm a little too shy to say that kind of stuff."

Rick pulled Mary close, and they shared a very long, very passionate kiss. The most passionate kiss since they had met in the diner. That meeting which seemed such a long time ago.

With their faces still inches apart, Rick whispered,

"Not bad for just good friends, hey?"

"Not bad at all," said Mary.

One more kiss goodbye.

"You drive safe."

"I will."

Rick took off for another long trip back to Augusta. The trips going away from Mary were certainly a lot longer than the ones going to see her.

CHAPTER 8
On Post Again

Rick arrived back on post late afternoon, giving him time to get over to Ed and Monika's place to drop off his diving gear and tools. Of course, Monika asked him to stay for supper, and he never turned that down, especially on Sunday night. Mess hall food on Sunday night was terrible. Monika made a nice batch of spaghetti, and wine was always available. They sat down and had a great evening meal together. Monika was busy cooking, but Rick could tell she was dying to ask how the weekend went. She waited until they sat at the table, but they had not sat down very long before she just blurted it out.

"All right, give us all the gory details of your weekend."

"Not too much to tell," said Rick quietly.

"Oh, come on, not too much to tell! All you talk about when you are with us is going down to see Mary. So, let's have it, buster. Did you kiss her, did you piss off the parents, can you ever go back, what?"

"I don't care about that shit." said Ed. "I want to hear about that piece of crap car, and did you get it going?"

"Ok, I give up," said Rick as he drank a big gulp of red wine.

Rick explained the whole weekend with Mary and her parents, in detail and probably with more excitement than they wanted to hear about Mary. He told Ed about the VW and how it turned out to be a very nice car after all. He spent a long time talking about the float down the river. More about Mary.

After answering all the many questions that Ed and Monika tossed at him, Ed about the car and river float, Monika all about Mary.

"How would you two like to make a road trip to Florida and meet Mary?"

"We are always up for a road trip," said Ed.

"And camping down in the swamps?"

"You know us, anything to get out of Augusta and away from the Army," said Ed.

"I'm not sure when as I haven't checked the duty roaster yet for next week," added Rick.

"A, I checked it," said Ed. "It will not be next weekend for you, buddy."

"Oh, great. What duty did I pull this time?"

"The good news is it is not guard duty. Well, maybe guard duty would be better."

"Ok, stop torturing me. What is it?"

"It is one that always provides good stories for us, and it is on Friday and Saturday night."

"No," Rick yelled. "Don't tell me it is the drunk-bus-run?"

"You got it, my friend."

"Shit," said Rick. "And no time off for that one either."

"Sorry, buddy, but better you than me."

The Army had made Rick go to big truck and bus driving training when he first got into the Army. He was qualified to drive the largest trucks and buses that the Army had. The drunk-bus-run was on Friday and Saturday nights where a bus went from Fort Gordon to downtown Augusta and back. It made a loop through all the seedy bars and clubs that cater to soldiers. Not to mention the prostitute section. The bars and the City of Augusta made an awful lot of money off these poor soldiers, so they looked the other way. Fort Gordon supplied a bus to bring the soldiers back and forth to keep them in line, out of jail, and off the streets.

Going to town was not too bad as they hadn't had much to drink. Coming back was another story as they were all drunk. Not to mention wholly obnoxious and some were downright mean. Fights would break out occasionally. Which was why an armed MP was always sitting up at the front of the bus with the driver. Rick always became very friendly and pleasant to the MPs. They had saved his ass many times. The other nice part was cleaning up after the GI's got sick from too much booze. Always a good time. The bus ran from 1800 hours to 0200 hours, so it was a long-ass night.

"I do have some good news," said Ed. "My CO called me in yesterday and said they are short one instructor for the next month. I mentioned you and he, for sure, would like to ask you to do the duty. Well, he is not really going to ask you, you know how the Army works, he will be telling you that you are going to do the duty."

"Oh, I see,"

"I hope you don't mind me mentioning you as I thought you would want it. It is an easy duty, and you know you get Fridays off for physical training."

"Now you got my attention, Ed," said Rick.

Rick knew that all the students had to do Army training on that Friday. Rick was a Non-Commissioned Officer (NCO), so he could do any physical training he wanted if he documented it well.

"That's good news," said Rick. "My PT can be anything, like diving, for example. I wonder where I could do that?"

"I thought you would be a happy soldier on this one," said Ed.

"Thank you, buddy. I owe you one. Not to mention that after a month of teaching, I will be really close to my discharge date."

"And no more having to kiss ass driving our lovely colonel around," added Ed.

"So, how about it?" Rick asked. "A week from Friday, do you want to head south for a little adventure?"

"Sounds like a good plan to me," said Monika.

"Adventures always good," said Ed.

They toasted with another glass of wine.

"I had better get back to the barracks and phone Mary before she goes to bed. Thanks for supper Monika," Rick said as he gave her a big hug.

"You are welcome, soldier."

"Thank you, buddy. I will probably see you tomorrow in the classroom," Rick said as he gave Ed a man hug.

Rick got back to the barracks, and fortunately, there was no one on the payphone. He put in his 25 cents and dialed Mary's number and got an operator right away. "Please deposit two dollars," said the voice over the phone line.

Rick put in his quarters.

"Hello," Joyce answered.

"Hi, Joyce, this is Rick. Is Mary close by?"

"I will put her on. Mary, come quick, it's Rick calling long distance."

"Hi Rick, you missed me already, didn't you?"

"Yes, I did, but not why I am calling. How about we do our river dive in two weeks. I have drunk bus duty next Saturday."

"Drunk bus duty?" Mary asked.

"Don't ask," said Rick. "I'll explain when I see you."

"I am going to be instructing so I can get there Friday sometime."

"Instructing?"

"Don't ask that either," said Rick. "Ed and Monika are up for coming also."

"Wonderful," said Mary. "It's crazy, but I do miss you already."

"In one minute, please deposit one dollar," interrupted the voice over phone line.

"I miss you also," said Rick as he speeded up his voice to beat the operator's clock. "I can't wait to see you in two weeks."

Mary speaking faster also, "I am so looking forward to our adventure and seeing you again. Goodbye, honey"

"Bye, Mary."

She called me honey, Rick thought. *That was nice and a first. Be careful here, Ricky boy. You will be out of the Army in a month and will be blessed with some major independence. You need to keep going forward with that plan. Let's not get tied down here.*

Ed was right. The following day, before Rick led the troops in morning PT, the company clerk came by with some freshly cut orders. He would be teaching an electronics course for the next month, over at the training center.

He was also hoping that he would get out of running the morning PT sessions, but no such luck. He was still going to be the company PT leader. This meant that he would have to get out of his work fatigues, shower, dress into his good khaki uniform, and then instruct new recruits about electronic stuff. It would make for a long day, but Fridays would be free.

Once Rick got into the morning PT and teaching routine, the week went fast, and because of the full days, he slept soundly every night. After finishing his Friday morning PT session, Rick met Ted at the Officer's Mess Hall. They had an excellent breakfast, much better than Rick would have gotten at his enlisted mess hall. Ted was a Lieutenant, so he could get Rick in. They were going to go out and play a round of golf for their PT session, so they were in civilian clothes and none of the officers knew Rick was an NCO. Ted liked his golf. Rick was not a real big fan, but it got him outside, and amazingly he was pretty good at it.

Friday night, drunk-bus-run started out slow, with not many troops going into town early. It was payday, so the post put two buses on, which always helped. Rick's MP was Dave. He seemed a nice guy, so they hit it off right away and got some excellent BS time in. There were many downtimes throughout the evening as they had to wait at the different bus stops. Dave used his MP radio to keep track of the other bus, which spread the routes out nicely. Of course, as the night got later, things got wilder and crazier. Both the bus and the soldiers got more loaded. Nothing drastic except for the offensive comments and noise level. No one blew lunch, so no clean-up. Rick was back in his bunk by 0200 hours and was asleep by 0202 hours.

Rick was able to sleep in on Saturday morning till 1100 hours, which he needed after the long week and drunk bus duty. He took a long breakfast in the mess hall with himself and Hemingway. By the time he got back to the barracks and took a shower, it was time to report at the motor pool again and pick up his bus. This bus was a bad one as the clutch was going out. The bus clutches were terrible anyway, as by the end of a shift, your leg was shaking from them being so hard to push to the floor. This bus was hard to shift a gear without some grinding. As more drunks got on board, every grind would send a cheer throughout the crowd. Dave was the MP again, so it made the night go faster and more tolerably between the two of them laughing about everything. Only three clean-ups, which after the crap bus he got, were not diligently executed.

On Sunday, Rick slept most of the day, so he was ready to go again by Monday morning.

Thinking of Mary and the upcoming adventure in the swamps kept Rick moving smoothly through the week. Thursday night, Rick got together with Ed and Monika over Monika's famous Shepherd's Pie. Rick checked his diving gear. He always kept a full tank of air. Everyone organized their camping equipment. Ed and Monika usually camped in their van, but Mary told Rick that they would not be able to drive to the campsite, so they would have to tent it. Monika offered to do all the food, which was nice.

The following day, Rick cut the physical training session drastically short and took a quick shower. Ed and Monika picked him up at the barracks and they were off for Lake City by 1000-hours.

CHAPTER 9
River Dive and Camp

Ed pulled the van into the diner parking lot and yelled, "Get up, soldier, we are here."

Rick woke with a jerk, "Ready," he said as he jumped from his horizontal position to a complete upright sit, bumping his head on the roof of the van.

Rick had been woken up so many times over the past three years with a sudden shock that it was just part of his nature now to get up flying and ready to go. The Army had trained him for that response, and it would be a long while before he would get over it.

"Here at your diner," Ed repeated.

"Oh," answered Rick.

Monika punched Ed on the shoulder from the passenger seat, "You are such a jerk, Ed. You knew that would freak him out."

"Sorry dear, it is a guy thing."

Rick got up, shook himself off, and brushed his hair back enough not to look slept on.

"I'll be right back."

He left the van and headed into the diner to meet Mary.

Mary was at the far end of the diner when Rick came through the door. She was delivering two plates of something to a booth table when she saw Rick. Quickly tossing the plates at the customers, Mary ran over to Rick. She jumped up and put her arms around his neck and gave him a big kiss. Mary was not thinking about anything or anyone around them in the diner. She was just happy to see him. For an instant, Rick felt a little uncomfortable, but when the old familiar excitement of seeing Mary kicked in, all his inhibitions melted away. It was just him and Mary there at the door.

"Hi," Rick said after their long embrace. "How are you doing?"

"Just fine, you big lug," Mary said as she stepped back from him and brushed her uniform with both hands to straighten out any wrinkles.

"I just stopped in to let you know that we were in town and heading for your house."

"Thanks, glad you guys made it OK. I will be off work at six. Just make yourselves at home. I don't think anyone will be home, so you'll have some time to rest before the inquisition starts."

"OK," Rick said. "As usual, you are looking pretty darn nice in that uniform, you know."

"Thank you, but any woman would look nice to one of you soldiers after looking at guys all week."

"You have a hard time with compliments, don't you?"

"I get them all day, so you are going to have to do better than that."

"I'll work on that then," Rick said.

A quick kiss, and Rick was heading back to the van.

At Mary's house, Ed parked his van on the concrete in front of the garage.

"I don't know how all of this is going to work," said Rick. "I just know that I will be sleeping up there, and Mary will be in the house over there, he pointed in both directions with his index finger."

"No problem," Ed said. "After this Army thing for the past three years, we're very flexible. We're fine here in the van if we can just use the bathroom."

"No problems," Rick said.

"The parents are very nice, a little strict, but very nice."

108

"They have to be strict with you around their daughter," Ed said with a smirk.

"I don't know what you are talking about, mister."

"Ed," Monika said, "You need to be extra nice and careful around these people. I have a feeling Rick really likes this lady."

"Thank you, Monika," said Rick, "At least I have one friend around here that understands things."

Ed just grunted.

"We will all be fine," Monika said.

Ed and Monika made up their bed in the back of the van and took a needed afternoon nap.

Rick went upstairs to his garage apartment, took another shower, and did the same in his bed. It seemed to him that the five-hour drive from Augusta was a lot longer when someone else was driving.

Rick was sleeping soundly when he felt a burning sensation on his nose. He opened his eyes, and Mary was tickling his nose with a pigeon feather she had picked up in the driveway. She was kneeling on the floor next to the bed. Her face was at eye level with Rick's when he turned his head and whole body towards her.

"You are such a nasty lady," Rick said while he rubbed his nose aggressively.

Mary quickly jumped up from the floor and onto the bed and snuggled next to Rick, facing him. She pushed her whole body into his so that every available point on each of them was touching.

Lying side by side and face to face, Mary said jokingly, "I am not a nasty lady, and don't you ever call me that again."

They shared a very warm and long kiss, amplifying every point that their bodies were touching.

They stopped their kiss, and with their faces still inches apart, Rick said softly, "Hi there, I missed you."

"I missed you." They kissed again.

"OK," Mary said as she jumped up out of bed and stood up next to it. "What is the plan here?"

"I don't know," Rick said as he came out of his excitement shock. "What do you think?"

"Well, mother is making supper for everyone, but our house is pretty small, so I am not sure about sleeping arrangements for your friends."

"No worries there as they like sleeping in their van."

"OK," said Mary, "That was easy."

"Have you met Ed and Monika yet?"

"No, it was pretty quiet in there when I went by."

"Well, let's go make it unquiet," Rick said as he jumped out of bed, grabbed Mary by the hand, and dragged her out to the van.

Banging on the side of the van, Rick yelled, "Hey, this is not a drill, front and center."

The sliding door slowly opened, and Ed and Monika rolled out and stood up next to the open door, eyes still half-open.

"Hey guys, this is Mary. Mary, Ed and Monika."

Mary quickly ran over to Ed, put her arms around his neck, and gave him a big hug, which opened Ed's eyes fully to a big round. She performed the same hug on Monika, who just looked over the top of Mary's shoulders at Rick and smiled.

"So glad to meet you, Mary," Monika said as they broke the hug. "We have certainly heard a lot about you. You are as pretty as Rick has said you were."

Mary and Rick were now both silent and blushing with heat.

Ed and Monika sat down on the edge of the van door opening while Mary and Rick stood in front of them. Rick leaned over to Mary and put his arm around her.

"So, what are we doing?" Ed said.

"I don't know," said Rick. "We need to ask our drill sergeant here, a, I mean tour guide.

"Very funny," said Mary as she hit Rick, a good slug on his arm.

"Well, my mother is going to cook us all supper because that is what she loves to do. From there, the only plan is to leave early in the morning for the river."

"Sounds like a good plan, drill sergeant, I mean Mary, a, tour guide," Ed said with a laugh.

Mary's mother had cooked a fantastic fried chicken meal with mashed potatoes, gravy, and corn on the cob. She did love to cook and was very good at it. The more people she was feeding, the better the potential for compliments and praise. She got her wish, as everyone expressed their appreciation over and over.

Everyone chipped in and helped clean up against Mary's mother's objections.

"It is a little early for you guys to turn in, so why don't you come up with us to Rick's apartment, and we can watch some TV," Mary said as they were approaching the van.

"Oh, it's Rick's apartment now, is it?" said Ed.

Monika hit him. "That would be great.".

They all went upstairs and squeezed together on the small couch. Mary brought the TV Guide and started looking at the evening's schedule.

"Let's see, it is eight o'clock... Oh, look, *Love American Style* is on right now."

A moan came from both Rick and Ed at the same time.

"Anything else," Rick asked.

"*Sanford and Son* and *The Odd Couple*," Mary read.

Sanford and Son, said Ed.

"I go along with that one," said Rick.

"Well, us girls want *Love American Style*." said Monika.

"Guess we will have to flip for it," said Rick, as he pulled out a quarter. "Heads or tails, ladies," as he tossed it into the air.

"Heads," said Mary.

"Damn," said Rick.

111

"How about best two out of three," said Ed.

"I think they got us," said Rick

They watched *Love American Style.*

Ed was unhappy, but Rick was delighted with his arm around Mary and her head gently leaning on his shoulder. The smell of her perfumed hair just inches from his face made for a lovely hour.

Ed and Monika went to their van.

Rick walked Mary to the bottom of his stairs and gave her a long kiss goodnight.

"That was very nice being with you tonight," he said. "Even if I had to share you with *Love American Style*, Ed , and Monika."

"Yes, it was," answered Mary as she touched his cheek and gave him another kiss.

"Good night, dear," she said as she walked towards the house. A few feet away she turned and said, "Maybe one of these days we can say good night, and neither one of us will have to go anywhere."

Rick got excited.

"Sleep well," he said.

The following morning, everyone was up at 0600-hours. Rick, Ed, and Monika because they were used to it, Mary, because that was what she liked to do. They loaded all the diving and camping gear into Ed's van, and after a quick breakfast, were off to the Ichetucknee River. Ed and Monika had taken care of all the food and drinks, so they didn't have to stop anywhere.

Mary directed Ed to the spot where she and Rick had parked his Jeep on their river floating adventure a few weeks earlier.

"We are at the headwaters of the Ichetucknee River," Mary said. "Rick and I have a little hike ahead of us, but if you would like to come along, I guarantee you will love it."

"And if they come, I bet they would love to help carry some of this diving gear, said Rick. "Plus, you could carry our shoes back."

"Oh yes," Mary said, "You need to wear shoes through here, the Sandspurs are nasty."

"We have nothing better to do," said Monika.

Ed just did another one of his grunts, "Two of my favorite things, hiking and carrying shit."

Ed started to pick up Mary's SCUBA tank, got it two inches off the ground, and dropped it back down again.

"I ain't carrying this thing for sure. These things are heavier than crap."

"You are such a wimp," said Monika as she picked up the tank and started carrying it along the path.

"Hey, Monika, you don't have to carry that," Rick said as he scooped it away from her grip. He had his tank on one shoulder and now Mary's on the other.

"I will get these if everyone else can get the other stuff."

Mary added, "And be sure and bring a couple of towels for you guys. You will want to swim in here for sure, trust me."

"She is so right," Rick said, "This is an amazing place to swim."

Mary led the group down the sandy trail with her mask, fins, and snorkel in her hands. Rick followed with the tanks, Monika had Rick's mask, fins, and snorkel and Ed carried the towels and two beers.

After the quarter-mile hike, they finally came to the opening that had impressed Rick the last time. It was precisely the same as he had remembered and dreamt about over the past few weeks.

"Here we are," said Mary as she tossed her gear on the limestone outcrop.

Rick tried to gently lower the two tanks to the ground, but he failed, and they fell to the rock with a loud clang.

"This is pretty cool," said Monika. "You were right, you guys."

"The water is fairly warm, so you guys can swim in here all afternoon if you want. There is usually no one around, so bathing suits are optional."

At that point, Ed perked up as he opened a beer, "I do believe a swim is in order."

"Please wait till we leave if you wouldn't mind," said Rick. "Monika would be lovely to see in the buff, but not you, Ed. I don't want to wake up in the middle of the night with that vision."

"I don't blame you," said Monika, "I have seen it in person."

"OK, you guys, I get the point."

"Just kidding, buddy," said Rick.

"I am not," said Monika, at which time Ed grabbed her, and they both stumbled into the water. They sat there in a foot of water and did a friendly kiss.

When they stopped, Ed yelled up to shore, "Don't you two need to get out of here."

"Hey, you need to come up here so I can explain to you where to set up camp," yelled Mary.

Ed and Monika slowly sloshed up the limestone rock as they were still both fully dressed in shorts, tops, and tennis shoes.

"Come over here, you two," Mary motioned them to a small area of wet sand where she was standing with a small stick in her hand.

She started drawing in the sand with the stick.

"We are right here at the headwaters," She drew a circle.

"Now, here is the Ichetucknee River," She drew a long squiggly line out of the circle.

"Rick and I are going to head out here," she pointed to where the squiggly line met the circle. Then she lifted the stick and pointed it across the pond. "That is that little opening you see over there."

She started running the stick down the squiggly line," The
River is going to wind for quite a distance here. This is the road
we came in on," Mary drew it in the sand.

"Take that back in the direction we came, back to Highway 47.
The first main road you come to, take a right and go all the way
down to Highway 27. Turn right on the highway and maybe two
miles. There is an electric substation on the right. There will be an
old dirt road that you will take a right off the highway, past the
substation. If you go past the river, you have gone too far. This
road is rough, so drive slowly. You will come to an opening in the
trees, and there will be another road. It is not really a road but a
two-rutted path. It was made by the railroad or power company
years ago. Think your van can make it, Ed?"

"My van will go more places than Rick's Jeep."

"OK then," Mary said. "This path will take you to another
opening. It's small, and there is barely room to turn around. Park
your van there. You will not see the river yet because it is thick
with trees and brush. The river is only about 100 feet from there.
Once you get out of the underbrush, you will see a nice little
beach. A good camping spot. Any questions?"

"How do you know all about these little secrets?" Ed asked.

"I am a local girl, you know. And I am not saying any more,"
as she glanced out of the side of her eyes at Rick.

"And I don't want to know," said Rick.

"Now, if we miss you there or you get lost, let's just wait for
each other at the Highway 27 bridge that crosses the river. If we
miss you there, we are on our way to the Santa Fe River and the
Gulf of Mexico, and it has been nice knowing you two."

Everyone did a nervous laugh.

"Got it," said Monika. "No problem."

Rick was impressed with Mary's knowledge and her
authoritative presentation. He got excited for an instant there until
Mary grabbed his hand and took him off to where their tanks were
lying.

"Come on, soldier boy, let's do this thing."

Rick and Mary helped each other strap on their tanks. Rick had his full-size tank, but Mary's was a smaller tank that fit her body frame better. They were both heavy out of the water but became light in the water. They decided not to bother with wet suits as the water was warm, and the river was not that deep so they would not be diving down into cooler water. Rick strapped his dive knife to the side of his calf, something he always carried as it had helped him out many times on past dives. They both placed their dive masks on top of their heads with the snorkels dangling to one side. Holding their swim fins in one hand and holding each other hands with their others, they walked across the limestone rock outcrop and into the water.

"You are looking pretty sexy wearing all that diving gear, my sweet," said Rick as he turned Mary towards him.

"Looking pretty good yourself, young man," said Mary.

Still holding hands, they pulled one another towards each other and attempted a kiss. Diving masks and snorkels got in the way, so they failed.

"Later, baby," said Mary. "Did you check your J valve?"

"I always do," said Rick. "I have some good stories when I have not. The outcome is never a good one."

"I know, I only left mine down once and had zero reserve," said Mary. "Fortunately, I was not very deep. Here turn around, and I will check yours just to make sure."

Rick's valve was up, and so was Mary's.

They sat down on the rock ledge in about three feet of water and put on their swim fins.

"This is a new adventure for both of us. How do you think we should do this?" Asked Mary.

"I am thinking we just snorkel and let the river carry us downstream, and whenever we feel like it, we change to tank and mouthpiece mode and go under. What do you think?"

116

"Sounds good to me," said Mary. "A lot of places will be pretty shallow and not worth using up the air on."

"See you guys downstream," yelled Rick at Ed and Monika. They both just did a quick wave as they had already taken half their clothes off for that naked swim.

"Crazies," Rick said, "But I love those two."

Rick and Mary both made a lunge forward from their sitting position and started bobbing in the water. The bottom dropped off quickly as they left the limestone bench, so they were floating almost immediately. They put their masks on while treading water, and before he placed his snorkel in his mouth, Rick asked, "Ready?"

"More than ready," answered Mary with a big smile.

They were floating immediately in about six feet of water.

Many chunks of rock had broken off the limestone shelf and were scattered on the bottom. There was very little vegetation among these rocks. The sand in around the rock chunks created an underwater passageway between them. The sun shining through the surface rippled created an eerie pattern on the rocks. Making them look almost like giant sponges.

Holding hands, they kicked towards the opening of the river on the other side of the pond. They passed through the familiar thick grasses coming from the bottom. The grass was so tall that it was almost touching them on the surface. As they approached the mouth of the river, the sides closed in. The narrow passageway into the river became very limited, with tall walls of vegetation surrounding them. The current seemed to pick up, and the floor became very deep.

Rick motioned to Mary with a finger pointing down. Mary nodded and took the snorkel out of her mouth and replaced it with her regulator mouthpiece. With a big blast of air bubbles from her regulator, she gave a thumbs up. Rick did the same, and they dove down to the sandy bottom. They held hands again and let the current glide them along the bottom. The sand was patched with

117

low-lying water plants that seemed to crawl along the river floor. Everything was a blue-green color. When they both looked up at the shiny surface, they faced each other, let go of each other's hand, and gave an enthusiastic thumbs up. With their mouthpieces in, you could not see, but they were both smiling. It was beautiful, and they both were at home.

The river widened and got shallow, down to a four-foot depth, so they surfaced and, without lifting their heads out of the water, changed back into snorkel mode.

They passed over a rocky area that looked like someone had dumped a whole load of brown rocks mixed in with the white limestone. They looked so out of place, and they were the size of baseballs. Rick did a surface dive down and picked one up and brought it back up to Mary. They looked at it while still snorkeling and their faces underwater. It was limestone but just a strange color. The brown rocks started getting smaller, ending up the size of quarters. A school of about ten panfish darted over the pebbles with their bellies almost touching them.

While concentrating on the panfish, Rick and Mary were stopped instantly with a muffled underwater thump, thump. Both of their heads had hit a large floating Mangrove tree that had fallen across the river. With their heads out of the water, they grabbed onto the tree trunk. They placed their masks on the tops of their heads at the same time.

"Ouch," Mary said.

"Are you OK," asked Rick.

"I am fine. It was just a shocker."

"I know, it sort of scared the shit out of me," Rick said.

"At least it was not a gator," laughed Mary.

"Now wait a minute, you said there were no gators on this river."

"I said I had never seen one, my dear."

"Oh, great, maybe I will let your head go just a little ahead of mine from now on."

"You are a big wimp," Mary said as she splashed Rick in the face with her free hand.

"It does say a lot for staying underwater more," said Rick.

"Yes, it does," said Mary. "Plus, less chance of bumping heads with a water moccasin also. They hang out on the surface, you know."

"Thanks again, my sweet."

"My dad said that the land snakes don't go underwater much, and if they do, they cannot open their mouths when in the water."

"Oh, that is so reassuring. Let's change the conversation."

"How about we stop at Blue Hole for a little rest?" Asked Mary.

"Sounds good."

"Remember, the river narrows just before Blue Hole, and there is that big bend. We stay right as left goes up into a big water pond area and another small river."

"It is your river. I trust you know the way."

The log stretched most of the way across the river, so they both just dove under it and continued snorkeling on the other side.

The river got deep again, so Rick motioned down, and they went into SCUBA mode again. Under the water was a again a happy place for both.

The long grass was now covering every inch of the river. It became wide and deep. Rick and Mary were moving along the west side of the river, along the steep walls of weeds. The other side of the river could not be seen, and the water was still extremely clear. With all the long, green vegetation, the water now had a green tinge to it. A large thirty-foot log stretched along the bottom. They swam just over the top of it. It had been there a while as it was covered with a thick layer of moss.

Mary and Rick were still holding hands as they swam maybe eight feet below the surface. Rick felt Mary give his hand a quick squeeze, so he looked over at Mary. Her eyes were big and white behind her mask lens. She gave a tiny nod with her head for Rick to look in the direction she was looking. Rick turned his head, and there was a three to four-foot Gar Pike swimming next to them. Rick looked back at Mary, and his eyes got big also. He nodded to Mary to look to her other side. She did. There was another Gar Pike swimming next to her. Then another came alongside that one. Two more swam over the top of them, coming only a couple of feet above their tanks. Mary squeezed Rick's hand a second time. Two in front and three on the sides. Rick looked back over his shoulder towards Mary, and there were another four Gars in the back of them. He motioned to Mary with his free hand for her to look back, and she did. Her eyes got big again. The Gars on each side were so close you could see their eyeballs sort of winking at them. The teeth on the long snouts were also winking at them.

They all swam together for a seemingly long time until they approached the small opening at the bend into Blue Hole. Rick squeezed Mary's hand and slowed their speed so the Gar could go ahead as the opening was deep but very narrow. The Gars just kept on swimming, and the four in the back glided over the top of them and joined the others. The whole group turned off to the left and went up another large tributary. They were gone as fast as they had showed up. The Blue Hole beach was straight ahead past the narrow opening. They swam up into the shallow waters to where they could stand up. Mary was the first out of the water and had her mouthpiece out and mask off instantly.

"Was that cool or what?" She said as she took off her fins and started heading up to the tiny little cleared area.

Rick followed, and they took off their tanks and sat down on the sandy ground.

Rick finally caught his breath.

"Yes, it was pretty amazing. I think those Gars thought we were just part of the family going out for a Saturday swim."

"They did not flinch or anything," said Mary. "I swear the ones on my side were smiling at me."

"I am sure they were. Probably the horny old males of the group. The ladies on my side were winking at me, so there."

"I was scared shitless when I saw the first one," said Mary.

"I hear you." Said Rick. "It is always an uncomfortable feeling when you are swimming in the water with something as long or bigger than you are. Then you toss in eight of them."

"Seeing some Manatees would really make our day," said Mary. "But they are not usually here in the summertime."

They sat at the Blue Hole beach, where they rested and warmed up for ten minutes.

"OK, we need to keep moving," said Mary. "We still have a long way to go. We do not have too many more places we can stop. It gets dense from here on down. After Mission Spring, the river will widen a lot and will have vegetation islands in the middle." We need to figure out which side is deeper as some channels get almost like a swamp. There is a landing after the wide area that we can stop if we want. It sure is harder getting bearings when we are in the water. I thought I knew this river like the back of my hand, but…"

"But?" Rick interrupted, "I do not want to hear no buts. You are my guide, remember, and I have no clue where we are going."

"I have a pretty good idea, dear. If you do see some brown-colored water, that means we hit the Santa Fe River, and we are on our way to the Gulf of Mexico."

As they put their diving gear back on, Mary asked, "Did you want to swim over by Blue Hole again? It is right here."

"I would like that," said Rick. "It was pretty darn cool.

Since we have our tanks, could we actually go into the opening a little way?"

"Maybe a little way," said Mary. "Not very far for me as I have a tough time in those spring things." I went into another spring with my boyfriend in high school, and it really freaked me out.

Just something about it does not sit well with me. I will wait for you at the opening."

"I understand," said Rick. "You are probably among the majority of the population with those feelings."

They waded back into the water until they were calf-deep and sat down on the sandy bottom to put their fin on. They tried an awkward kiss again with their masks on top of their heads, but it did not go well.

"We need to work on that one, don't we," said Rick.

"Yes, we do."

They lunged forward into the water belly first and were once again floating together.

They had been around a slight bend from Blue Hole, so it was a very short swim. The hard part was negotiating some floating vegetation at the mouth of the inlet. Some of the plants collected on their heads and face masks. When they were above the Blue Hole opening, they switched to their SCUBA mouthpieces and, while holding hands, dove the twenty feet down to the Blue Hole spring opening. It looked very familiar as it was only a few weeks ago that they had been floating above it in Puffy. It was just as strange looking this time. The big dark circle with a larger circular sandy border. These circles were then framed by another ring of green, a vast field of long, green grasses. It did so look like a giant eyeball. Rick and Mary both dove down to the rim of the spring, where Mary waited on her knees on the sandy bottom. The grasses were being whipped around violently by the current. Rick squeezed Mary's hand slightly and did a quick thumbs up. He then headed down into the spring. He had no light or safety lines, so he was not going to go in very far. Rick wanted to go in far enough to look up and see the light coming through the opening. Something he had remembered from his other cave dives as being the most impressive part. The current was intense, and with minimal weights on, Rick had to kick hard to get down far enough. He finally made it down into the spring about twenty feet and was exhausted. It opened into a larger area, so Rick could turn around and look back out the opening. As he remembered in his other cave dives, it was so beautiful as the light got filtered through the blue water and reached down into the cave as separate slivers of brightness. The contrast between the black background of the cave walls and the green algae in the water amplified the beauty. Rick loved it. He didn't stay long and swam out and joined Mary, where she was still kneeling in the sand. He gave her a happy thumbs-up, and they surfaced. Treading water on the surface above the spring, Rick took his mouthpiece out first and said, "Thank you, Mary, for waiting. That was pretty cool."

"You are welcome. Glad you got in there."

They decided to stay underwater, so they put their mouthpieces back in, held hands, and started floating down the river again.

The river was wide after the spring, with mostly vegetation and very little exposed sand on the bottom.

Even though it was all the same river, the variety of everything was a constant change. There was always something new. There seemed to be more fish and different varieties of them in the section after the Blue Hole. Fish would dart in and out of their hiding places, coming out briefly just to say hello and then flashing back into their cover.

Mary let go of Rick's hand and pointed up. They surfaced and treaded water in the middle of the stream. Mary took out her mouthpiece and said, "Mission Spring is just up ahead, and there is a small beach there. Did you want to stop again?"

Rick took his mouthpiece out of his mouth, "I am fine to keep going. How about you?"

"That is good for me," said Mary. "How about we stay under for a while? I cannot get enough of it down there."

"I hear you, girl."

They did a test blow on their mouthpieces and dove down to the bottom.

Past Mission Spring, the River widened a lot and then split into two tributaries. Fortunately, it was obvious which was the main route and the deepest. It narrowed again to a point where the two of them had little room on each side. The mangrove roots were stretching down to the river bottom like giant spider webs on one side. On the other was a vast wall of vegetation, going straight up to the surface. Mary was swimming on the mangrove side when she squeezed Rick's hand with a quick jerk. She pointed with her other hand in the direction of the tree roots next to her. Four feet away was a large copperhead snake weaving in and out of the mangrove roots. It had to be at least two feet long but looked six. It had its mouth wide open. Mary looked back at Rick with her big eyes and started kicking harder, still holding hands. Rick did the same.

The river instantly got very wide. Mary pointed up, so they surfaced in the middle of the river again. Treading water, they both scanned the surface around them. The river was wider now. Maybe the width of a football field. The walls of vegetation on the sides were equally vast. Pulling her mouthpiece from her mouth and pushing her mask on top of her head, she just said, "I don't want to talk about that copperhead right now."

"OK," said Rick.

Mary did continue talking, however, "So much for my dad's knowledge of snakes. Did you see it was underwater, and it had its mouth open?"

"Yes, I did."

"OK, now that is all I am going to say about the snake."

Rick could tell she meant it, so he didn't say anything.

"The opening of the river will stay wide here, but the channel will get a lot smaller. We must make sure we stay in the main river or things will get very thick and sloppy. It is bad enough floating in Puffy, so I cannot imagine swimming through it. They don't call it Grassy Hole Spring for nothing, you know. Oh, and it will get really shallow in some spots."

"You are the guide, my little mermaid."

Mary rolled her eyes and they both snorkeled-up, and started floating again.

Mary was right. The vegetation was all around them, and at many points, it got so shallow that they were rubbing their bellies on the bottom weeds. Once again, they were getting vegetation parts on their heads and masks when swimming off course into the side areas. Rick had thoughts, that he tried to ignore, of swimming headfirst into a floating water moccasin or alligator. He just held Mary's hand a little tighter and hoped she did not have the same thoughts. They had to stop a few times to get bearings when they came to where the river seemed to divide. It was always not obvious which way was the mainstream now. At one point in the shallows, where their bellies were rubbing the bottom vegetation, they were almost flopping like salmon going upstream to get through it. At another point, Mary really squeezed Rick's hand very hard and almost jerked his arm off. When he looked over at her, she had her big eyes again, but she just smiled behind her mouthpiece.

The wide area was short-lived, maybe fifteen hundred feet, and they were back on the narrow river again. Fortunately, the depth increased again. It was still shallow and not worth going under, but they were not rubbing bottom with their stomachs.

They just floated and floated. Every inch of the river supplied a new view of something. The variety of it all was beautiful. Swimming in the river gave Rick and Mary a sense of being part of it and not just observers. Before they knew it, they had arrived at the small landing area where Mary's dad had picked them up with Puffy. They had decided that they would stop there and rest before they made their final float to where Ed and Monika would, hopefully, be waiting for them.

The landing was a lovely sandy beach area with a lot of large limestone rocks scattered everywhere. The stones were all covered with green moss. The trees were tall like everywhere else along the river, but they were more spread out. You could see sky and sunlight through them. They floated onto the shallow area and stood up in two feet of water. They knew they would not stay long, so they left their fins on and just walked backwards up to the beach. With tanks still on, they sat close to each other on the sand with their fins still half-submerged. They took off their masks and looked at each other.

"How are you doing?" asked Rick.

"I am doing great, and you?"

"Wonderful. Nothing against old Puffy, but this is the only way to float this river."

"Don't tell Puffy, but I have to agree with you."

"How much farther?" Asked Rick.

"We are pretty close," Mary said. "Maybe another thirty minutes. The river bottom will fill with white sand just before we get to where we will get off the river and hopefully meet Ed and Monika. The white sand will be our sign that we will be getting close. I think we might be done with our underwater diving as it stays shallow from now on. Glad we went under as much as we did as I like the headwater section better than this stretch."

They sat in the warm sun for a short while, just watching the river.

"Pretty darn cool," Rick said as he leaned over and gave Mary a very long kiss.

Breaking from their kiss, they just looked at each other for a second, "Just saying," Rick added.

"I do have something to tell you," Mary said very slowly.

"Am I going to like this?"

"Well, remember when I sort of squeezed your hand back there in that heavy weeded area?"

"You mean when your eyeballs looked like ping pong balls."

"They did?"

"Yes, they did."

"And remember when I said that I had never seen a gator on this river before?"

"Yes."

"Well, I cannot say that anymore."

"You are kidding me," said Rick. "Why didn't you tell me back there?"

"I don't know, I should have, I guess I…."

Rick didn't let Mary finish, "I am sort of glad you didn't, especially after our heads got covered with all the floating river weeds."

"I was a little freaked out," said Mary.

"How big was it?"

"Maybe four feet. It was just minding its own business swimming on the surface."

"All part of the adventure, my dear," Rick said as he gave Mary another short kiss.

"OK, let's bring this adventure on home," added Mary.

They turned around and backed into the water and snorkeled downstream again. The river was mostly all vegetation on the bottom now. Rick and Mary had to stay in the center of the river as the sides got shallow very quickly.

Mary was right. The bottom instantly turned into white sand with just a scattering of vegetation. The sides were still covered with water weeds, but the center was like a guiding landing strip. They rounded a sharp bend in the river, and within a few hundred feet, Mary pulled on Rick's hand, and they stopped in the middle of the river to look around.

They were a little later than expected with all the stops. Rick could tell that Mary was getting a little anxious as they got closer to the take-out point. They both knew if they missed it, they would be floating downstream for miles before Ed and Monika would realize it. They could end up at the Santa Fe River. So, they stopped, put their heads above water, and looked at the surrounding riverbanks very carefully. Mary was having trouble getting her bearings as to where they were. She knew there would be a tiny beach area, but it was just after a bend in the river, so it would be easy to miss. They had just gone around a bend, so it could be close. They saw only vegetation on both sides of the river, so they returned underwater. Holding Mary's hand, they continued to float downstream. Looking over at Mary, he could see that her eyes through the glass of her facemask were telling him that she was getting concerned. He felt her also peeking above the waterline to look continuously. A large glob of vegetation hit Rick's face, which caused him to stop and put his head above the water. The water and vegetation slid down the front of his mask. When his view was restored, a beach appeared in his vision like a divine inspiration. *Could this be the take-out spot?* He wondered. Mary, sensing Rick stopping in the water, put her head above the waterline and saw the same beach. She pulled her snorkel out of her mouth and said, "We did it. This is the beach. You are so good, Rick." Rick said nothing as he had no clue how they got here or what he had done.

They left the center of the river and swam towards the beach on the left side. They had to fight the current to get a path to the beach without floating farther downstream. Their stomachs started rubbing the sandy bottom, which was a good indicator that they were on the shallows of the beach and could stand up at any time. Rick planted a knee in the soft sand and then his other knee. He got enough of a knee-hold in the sand to raise himself up into a standing position, which always felt so nice after floating for hours in the water. Rick grabbed Mary by the underside of her armpits and lifted her out of the water. They both were now standing in two feet of water. Smiling at each other, they started to walk to shore. They were halted quickly when their swim fins hit the rushing water and sand resistance, and they both stumbled back into the water. With their heavy tanks and weight belts, it was a fast trip down. Rick caught himself, but Mary did a face-plant onto the water surface. Laughing and still holding her hand, Rick yanked her back to her feet.

"You are such a klutz, girl," Rick said, "Didn't they teach you in diving school that you walk backward with swim fins on in the water."

As Mary shakily got back on her feet, she said, "Thank you for your help and your kind words, you jerk." Mary started to hit Rick with her free hand, but Rick caught it in mid-air. He grabbed it tightly and spun her around, which would have been a very smooth move, but his foot caught in the sand, and they both went crashing into the water again. Rick hit the water first, and Mary followed, landing right on top of him. Face to face, they paused and looked at each other before they shared a kiss. It was a long and passionate kiss amplified by the flowing, crystal clear water and white sand. It was lovely but short-lived as the weight of Mary, and her tank on Rick, plus his tank digging into his back, was overpowering the excitement of the kiss.

"Hey, you two!" came a loud voice from the shore. "Get a room. This is a family beach, and some people here were getting worried about you kids."

It was Monika on the beach, standing there with both hands on her hips like a disturbed mother. Her brightly colored red bikini stood out against the green vegetation and the white sand beach.

Rick and Mary halted their embrace and gave each other a disappointed look. They sat up in the shallow water and removed their fins and walked towards Monika on the shore.

They did a group hug.

"About time you got here, we were starting to worry that you were already in the Gulf of Mexico. Camp is all set up, and Ed is out trying to find some firewood."

Monika was right. They had set up their tent and built a fire ring for a campfire. Campfires are not for warmth in Florida but are the only way to keep the insects from eating you alive after the sun goes down.

"We didn't set up your tent because we are not that nice."

Rick and Mary's gear was lying in a pile way off to one side of the campsite. Nothing was in order, just a large pile of gear.

"Thank you," said Rick. "You guys, just being here is more than enough.

Mary and Rick walked over to the pile of gear and just stared at it for a few minutes until Mary finally said, "I guess it is not going to set itself up, is it."

"You are so smart dear, I guess we should help it."

They started the usual unpacking and setting up camp.

Mary tossed out the sleeping bags. This time of year, it was scorching in Florida, so sleeping bags were not needed, but Rick always carried them as they made a nice cushion against the hard ground.

"Tent first," said Rick as he dumped out all the tent parts on the ground. Rick had set up so many tents in his life that he had it up before Mary got over to help him. While Rick finished the tent, Mary spread out the sleeping bags inside and made a bed on top with some old sheets and pillows. Mary had made it very clear that she had to have a pillow. Rick was happy with a rolled-up shirt, but she had insisted. He did, however, find them a very nice luxury in the wild when he used them.

Finally, things were organized. Mary grabbed Rick's hand. "let's go take a look at this beach," Mary said as she dragged Rick off to the water.

It was a tiny river beach. Maybe 30 feet long and 10 feet deep. It was surrounded by very dense vegetation, so thick that there would be no way to pass through it without a good machete. Most of the vegetation was short shrubs and bushes. Away from the river, there were scattered magnolia trees that were over 20 feet tall. It was all impassable except for a small pathway where the water met the sand at the far end.

The vegetation went all the way to the water on both sides of the beach, giving it a definite private feel. As far as could be seen, on the other side of the river was also dense vegetation. They were for sure alone.

Monika yelled out across the small beach. "You two get over here and have some cold Boone's Farm Strawberry Wine."

Ed returned from his firewood gathering, and when he saw Rick and Mary, his wood was dropped, and he came running towards them. He smashed into each of them with outstretched arms and gave them a healthy hug. "So glad to see that you two made it OK. We thought you might be speaking Spanish in Mexico by now."

They all headed back through the soft sand to the camp. Ed and Monika's tent was off to the side, with the fire at the center. Monika was holding a large pot over the coals at the end of a large stick.

"A one-pot meal tonight, kiddies, Hungarian goulash." Ed had stacked up enough wood to build a house, and the fire was going crazy. Ed prided himself in his fire building. Obsessed with it at times, but he was good at it.

Mary let loose of Rick's hand and turned and gave him a short kiss on the cheek.

"I am going to help Monika. You two build fire, ug." She said in a broken caveman tone.

As she walked away, Rick could not take his eyes off what was moving inside that bikini. His gaze was interrupted by Monika passing Mary with a bottle of Boone's Farm and two glasses.

"A little beverage, boys?"

"Thank you, honey," said Ed.

"You can just leave the bottle, lady," said Rick.

"But of course, boys," Monika said, as she turned and amplified her walk away, swinging her red bikini.

131

"So how was the float, Rick?" said Ed as he sipped his strawberry wine.

"It was amazing, Ed. The water was so clear, and taking the tanks was a great idea. When we have more time, I will have to tell you more about some great stuff, especially diving with the gear."

"Hey, you guys, supper is on the table, well, blanket," called Monika.

The girls had set up a blanket in the sand with a lighted candle at the center. Four bowls of Hungarian goulash were placed on each side. Next to the candle were napkins and a large bowl of bread. Mary and Monika were sitting at each corner. Rick sat next to Mary.

"Hi dear, long time no see," Mary said, as she softly put her hand on his bare leg. Rick did not complain as it made him feel very warm and excited.

Rick raised his glass and said, "Here is to a great float today and especially to good friends. Thank you so much, you two, for helping us enjoy the day."

They clanged their plastic glasses together, which turned out more of a *thud* than a *clang*.

The cold, pink wine tasted so delicious after a long day in the sun and in the hot evening air. Everyone immediately dug into the goulash. It was an excellent meal, as all food tastes so great out in the open air. The supper went on with the usual laughter, fooling around, and general silliness for two hours. What always happened when anyone got together with Ed and Monika. It was a perfect end to a wild and crazy day.

"OK," said Rick. "It has been a very long day, and we need to get up early in the morning for that long trip back to our reality, called Fort Gordon."

Rick got up on his feet and grabbed Mary's hand, pulling her up off the blanket.

"Don't worry about the clean-up. We have it covered. We have not done anything all day, so we can handle it, right Ed?", Monika declared.

Ed reluctantly said, "Yes, dear"

"You two get some needed sleep," Monika said

Ed followed with another "Good night, you two."

"Thanks again, guys," said Mary, as she grabbed Rick's hand and turned him towards their tent.

Rick and Mary climbed down into the small tent opening, which was always an adventure-in-tself. He quickly zipped up the screen flap.

"The fire kept those nasty mosquitos away, but they are going to find us very soon over here. It is going to stay pretty warm tonight, so I think we should keep all the flaps open, don't you."

"For sure," said Mary. "It is Florida, you know."

Rick hung a portable battery-powered light at the top of the tent which gave a warm orange glow as it reflected off the tent sides. It was not a bright light, but it gave off enough light to arrange things.

Mary and Rick had agreed ahead of time that this would just be a friendly camping trip, and each would have their own sleeping space. Mary had also promised her mother that this was just a camping trip with friends and that things would be friendly and innocent. Both Rick and Mary fully agreed that this is how it should be. So, without much conversation, they both made up their own little bed. On each side of the tent. The sleeping bags were underneath, which made for an excellent barrier from the hard sand. Rick had brought two full-sized sheets to share. One on the bottom next to the sleeping bags and one for over the top of them.

Mary was still in her bikini swimsuit, so she grabbed the top sheet and crawled under it and took off her bikini bottoms and replaced it with her short, short sleeping pants. She removed her bikini top and slid into an old surfing tee shirt. Her usual sleep wear for as long as she could remember.

She pulled the soft top sheet up around her neck and spoke. "I am now ready for some sleep."

"That was quick," said Rick. "You can really move when you put your mind to it."

Mary stretched one arm from under the sheet and hit Rick on the shoulder.

Rick was still in his bathing suit, and he usually slept with nothing on. Out of respect for things, he was just going to sleep in an old pair of oversized boxer shorts. Under his side of the top sheet, he slipped out of his bathing suit and quickly replaced it with the old striped boxers.

"Whew, that was a lot of work," said Mary.

"Yes, it was," answered Rick.

"Just to get ready for bed."

Silence overcame the tent as they both lie on their backs under the cool sheet. The tent was glowing from the embers in the dying campfire. They both stared at the tent walls for a long while.

"Thank you for a wonderful trip down the river, Mary."

"You are so welcome, my dear. Sharing it with you made it complete."

"Hope you sleep well," said Rick, as he rolled over to give Mary a good-night kiss.

She rolled over at the same time to give him the same. They did a short peck on each other cheek, then a quick kiss on the lips as Rick gently touched Mary's cheek. They both backed away and looked into each other's eyes for a moment. Mary then softly touched Rick's cheek with her free hand that was above the sheet. Rick felt the softness and warmth of her hand on his face. She held her hand on his cheek while they did one more kiss.

"Good night, my dear," she said as she raised her hand from his cheek to a gentle touch on his temple. Then she ran all her fingers through his hair just above his ear. She then slowly made the same motion to the back of his head. Finishing with a firm grip at the back of his neck. She pulled Rick closer, and they shared another goodnight kiss. Still enjoying the long last kiss. Rick gently moved his hand to the back of Mary's head and gently stroked her soft hair with feather-light fingertips. His fingers ran through her silky hair. Hair that was still stiff from a day in the water but still soft as silk. His hands then flowed to the back of her neck, pulling her lips closer to his and turning a light kiss into one of higher heat and passion.

They both stopped at the same time after a long passionate moment.

"We were going to keep this a friendly relationship, remember," whispered Rick. "You did promise your mother, you know,"

"I did."

Mary lifted the sheet up and rolled over under the sheet toward Rick's side of the tent. They now were facing each other, close enough that each could feel the other's heat through the skimpy sleeping garb.

After a long moment of enjoying the warm feel of each other, Mary crawled out from under the sheets. She could not stand in the small tent, so she pulled off her sleeping shorts in one swift motion while lying on her back. She then slowly removed her cotton top. Rick was watching Mary's lovely dance from under his sheet. Mary crawled over and dropped down on top of Rick and gave him a long and passionate kiss. Rick felt her naked body through the sheet and got very excited. Mary rolled off the top of Rick, pulled the sheet off him, and gently pulled off his boxers.

Mary settled her body back down on top of Rick. They shared a very long kiss. A passionate kiss. A degree of passion that neither one of them had ever felt before.

Their bodies were now as close as they could get without melting into each other. They exchanged another hot and passionate kiss.

With their faces still so close and after a long pause, Mary whispered, "You do realize that I am falling in love with you, don't you Rick."

"I know," said Rick. After a much longer pause than Mary's, he finally answered, "and I do believe it is working both ways here. I am falling in love with you also."

They both felt the love growing between them, and the passion took over. They did keep Mary's promise to her mother, not wholly, but they did keep it. They just enjoyed each other and pleased each other throughout the night. They fell asleep in each other's arms but not before a final expression of their newly found love for each other was expressed again.

The hot Florida sun started its heat dance on the tent walls very early. A built-in tent alarm clock.

Mary had fallen asleep with her head on Rick's chest where she did not move throughout the night. The tent heat woke Mary up first. She raised her head slightly enough to notice that their naked bodies were still tightly wrapped under the sheets. Mary felt warm and glowing, and she knew it was not from the hot Florida sun beating on the tent walls. She smiled as she gently woke Rick with a soft kiss on his cheek. Rick opened his eyes slowly, opening them to see those gorgeous brown eyes looking at him, framed by her long hair on his face.

"Good morning," Mary said as she gave Rick another soft kiss on his cheek. She then lifted herself up and rolled over on top of Rick. They had not bothered to get dressed in the middle of the night, so they were both still naked. The flesh on flesh felt so lovely and natural for both.

"Good morning, my dear," Rick said, looking into Mary's eyes.

Before Rick could say some words that he wanted to say the night before…"Coffee and breakfast are done," Monika yelled as she was walking towards their tent.

"Shit, Monika is coming," said Rick.

Mary whispered as she rolled off Rick's body, "And you know she will peek through the screen to say good morning."

In one swift motion, Mary had her halter top on and was lying on her back on the other side of the tent. Rick had his t-shirt on at the same lightning speed and escaped to his side of the tent. They did not have time for their bottom halves, so they both quickly crawled under the sheet.

Looking at Rick's t-shirt, Mary said, "Nice shirt you have there, fella. Too bad you have it inside out."

"Crap," Rick said as he fixed the problem in one swift motion.

They both did a little school kid giggle and gave each other a handshake across the tent. Good timing, as Mary was right, Monika peeked through the screen at that moment.

"Are you two decent in there?"

"Of course, we are," said Rick. "We would not think of being anything else."

They both fought back another giggle.

"We agreed we all needed to get up early to pack up and hit the road, my dear soldier boy. Remember we have to be back on post before 1700 hours as Ed must report for the week's roster."

"OK, mother," Rick said as he looked to make sure Monika was leaving.

As Monika turned to walked away, Rick and Mary did a synchronized jump out from under the sheets and were into their bathing suit bottoms as fast as they had gotten out of them the night before.

"Now we are decent and legal again," said Mary.

Rick unzipped the bug screen and climbed out of the tent. He stood up and put out his hand to Mary.

"Let's go, my lady."

Mary grabbed his hand, and with one motion, Rick lifted her to her feet and into his arms.

"Hi there," Rick said as he gave her a short, warm kiss.

Still holding hands and staying very close, they walked over to the burned-out campfire where Ed and Monika were sitting. Monika was pouring two cups of coffee for them as they approached. As Monika handed them their coffees, she looked at Rick and then at Mary. Monika had a big smirk on her face. She knew.

"Did you two sleep well?" Monika said with a little sarcastic tone.

"Wonderfully," said Mary.

"What's for breakfast? I am starved," Rick said to change the subject.

"Oatmeal with raisins and some glazed donuts for dessert," answered Ed.

"My kind of breakfast," Rick answered back quickly.

They spent an hour hanging out and eating breakfast. Rick had to bring up Mary's alligator, of course. The rest of the time was a lot of laughter, something they all knew how to do well.

After breakfast, everyone tore down tents and cleaned up the campsite. They were on the road and on the way back to Mary's house within an hour. It was a major operation unloading SCUBA gear and camping equipment into the garage at Mary's house. Ed and Monika waited in the van for Rick as he said his goodbyes to Mary.

"Thanks for a very fun trip," Mary said as she put her arms around Rick's neck.

Rick brought Mary in close, so their faces were only inches apart, and said, "It was pretty darn nice, wasn't it?"

"I will miss you," said Mary.

"I will miss you also," Rick said as he smiled a little. "I also have a nice surprise for you."

"Now? you are going to give me a surprise as you are leaving?"

"Yes, I am. Guess who does not have any duty next weekend?"

"Really!" said Mary as she kissed Rick on the lips. "So, you can meet me and Linda in Atlanta?"

"You betcha, sweetheart," Rick said, doing a pretty good Bogart.

"That is so wonderful and a very nice surprise."

They did a long and passionate kiss.

"I am a pretty happy girl, you know."

"Yes, I do, and I am a pretty happy guy."

"See you in Atlanta, baby," Rick failed at Bogart this time.

Rick was on his way back to Augusta once again. He was really missing Mary this time, and he knew she was missing him. They had just made a giant leap forward.

CHAPTER 10
Atlanta

It was Friday morning, and Rick was up at his usual 0600-hours and on the parade field with the company troops by 0630 hours. He was ready to get the physical training over so he could get an early start on the road to Atlanta. Generally, on a Friday, Rick would cut every activity shorter than usual anyway. There were never any complaints from the troops when he did. In fact, they loved him for it. He slept with all these guys, night after night, so he knew them all well.

Rick called everyone to fall in, and he started them on the usual warm-up jumping jacks. Halfway through the fifty counts, Rick noticed off to the side of the parade field was the posts physical training officer with his flunky clerk. The clerk, of course, had a clipboard and pen in his hand.

"Shit," Rick mumbled under his breath. "Of all fucking mornings, and I get a goddamn PT inspection."

Usually, he never made the troops count out loud because he thought it was stupid. Today, however, he gave the order as they dropped for push-ups, "on my count, 1, 2, 3..."

Everyone went along as word spread quickly throughout the company that the higher-ups were watching. After the 50 push-ups, the 100 sit-ups were next. Rick never pushed the 100 goals, but today he had no choice. Everyone in the company followed along. 100 sit-ups later, they were ready for the next movement of pain.

Usually, the two-mile run was at the end of the main workout, but Rick thought, *enough of this shit.*

"Close ranks. Left face."

Rick quickly ran to the side of the company.

"Forward. March. Double time"

The company started running off to the other end of the parade field. Usually, they just ran around the parade field, but Rick took them off the parade field and out into the street.

Rick figured the jar-heads, what he called officers in charge, would not hang around till they got back. He was correct, as when he looked back, they were already heading off the parade field.

After about only a mile, Rick gave the command, "Company halt. About face. Forward march. Double time."

They headed back to the parade field. On the parade field, the company all lined up for the rest of the physical training.

Rick stood in front of them and yelled, "Company dismissed."

There was a silence, then a loud cheer until Rick motioned with his one hand to calm down. It was instantly quiet, and everyone ran back to the barracks, followed by Rick, walking.

Rick was now able to get in his Jeep and off to Atlanta by mid-morning. It was only a two-hour drive, so he arrived at the Peachtree Hyatt Regency a little before noon. Rick wanted to get there early as Mary had said they were shooting for an early afternoon arrival. He had made reservations for a room the week before and was shocked at the price. He wanted an east-facing room as he loved to see the sunrise in the morning and one higher up with a view.

He walked into the lobby and was amazed and in awe as much as he was the first time he had been there. He and a few Army buddies went to the Peachtree a couple of years ago on leave. They did not stay at the Peach Tree but had drinks in the rotating bar on the roof. They rode the elevators up and down until they were asked to leave. Then they went back to their cheap motel on the west side. He hoped this time would be different as a paying

141

customer. It was a fantastic place, ahead of its time in design. The entrance from the street was a long tunnel that gradually narrowed toward the lobby. Emerging from the tunnel into the atrium was like being outside. The ceiling was twenty floors above the main floor, and all the hallways to the rooms were wrapped around the center area. Live plants hung from each balcony on every floor and actual tall trees were growing in the lobby. The live vegetation amplified the outdoor ambience. Large tiles arranged in a fan pattern over the entire lobby floor provided disorientation of a different sort. Nature-themed giant sculptures stood randomly around the lobby. A sizeable floating birdcage bar covered one whole corner of the square lobby floor. The top was open, like a birdcage, so you could look up into the hotel. The most striking feature of the place was the three pod-shaped elevators. They traveled on the outside of large columns that went from the main floor to the roof. They were all glass with bright lights highlighting each of them.

Mary is going to so love this, Rick thought.

Rick went to the desk to check-in. He looked a little out of place with his jeans, sandals, and Hawaiian shirt. More noticeable was his Army duffle bag that he always traveled with. The lady at the desk was very friendly and said that check-in was not until three o'clock, but she could have his room ready in an hour. He told her that he was expecting some other guests and that he would be waiting in the bar.

Rick walked towards the elevator column and into the birdcage bar floating right in front of the elevators. The cage was above the floor, so he had to climb up into it. Rick found a small table towards the outside, looking out over the lobby and front desk. He could see when Mary and Linda would arrive. He tossed his duffle under the small round table and sat down in a very plush leather chair with high armrests. Behind him was a giant birdcage that covered a good portion of the center area. In it were some very colorful parrots that were just sitting on a large branch. There was no one else in the bar except the bartender, so Rick walked over to the bar and ordered a beer. Back at his table, he settled in and took a long look around at the fantastic surroundings. He then pulled out Hemingway's *Death in the Afternoon* and sipped his beer in between turning pages.

After over an hour had passed, Rick looked up and saw Mary and Linda coming through the tunnel. There was also another woman with them. Rick had already finished his beer, so he just had to toss his book in his duffle bag, sling it over his shoulder, and head out of the bar down into the lobby. Linda was already at the desk checking in, and Mary was looking up at the ceiling. She happened to look over in Rick's direction and saw him coming across the tiled floor. A big smile spread across her face, and, grabbing her bag, she walked briskly over to meet him.

Before either said a word, they dropped their bags and did a stiff embrace, followed by a lovely short kiss.

"Do I know you, ma'am," said Rick.

"No, but I bet you would like to, wouldn't you?"

They looked at each other for a second, picked up their bags, turned, and headed over to where Linda was standing at the desk.

"Well, hi there, Rick," Linda said as she walked over to Rick and gave him a big hug. "So nice to see you again."

She turned and grabbed the other lady's hand and led her to where Rick and Mary stood.

"This is my friend Susan who decided to come along at the last minute."

"Nice to meet you, Rick. I've heard a lot about you."

"Nice to meet you," Rick answers back. "I guess a lot of talking can go on with that long drive up here. I wondered why my ears were ringing."

"I bet they were," Susan answered back with a quick glance over at Mary.

Mary blushed.

"Have you ever been here before?" Susan asked Rick.

"Yes, a couple of my Army buddies came over here a while back and sort of snuck in here, rode the elevators up and down a few times, and hung out up in the Polaris restaurant until they kicked us out."

"So, you didn't stay here?"

"No, we went over to Uncle Sam's, a bar where they had five-cent beers, and then drove back to our fleabag hotel over on the west side. Hey, I could take you all over to Uncle Sam's if you want!" Rick said with fake enthusiasm.

Linda was pretty sure Rick was kidding but just in case he wasn't, she said, "How about we get back to you on that one."

Linda and Susan turned and walked back over to the check-in, where the desk lady was waiting for them.

Mary grabbed Rick's hand and turned to look up into the hotel lobby.

"This is pretty amazing," she said. "I need to get out of Lake City more often."

Rick looked over at Mary, and her eyes were as big as they had been when she saw that gator on the river.

"It's pretty impressive, isn't it? A little nicer than your dad's garage apartment."

"A little bit," Mary said. "Don't tell him that, however. He is proud of that garage apartment."

With room keys in her hand Linda came over to where they were standing.

"Can you believe it? They let us check in early! Have you checked in yet, Rick?"

Rick just reached in his pocket and pulled out his keys, dangling them in the air.

"What room are you all in?" Rick asked.

"You all, you have been hanging out in the south a little too long, boy," Linda said with a chuckle. "We are on the 12th floor, and you?"

144

"I am up on the 16th. Did you guys just get one room?"

"At these prices, you are kidding me, right?" Linda answered back. "One room with two double beds."

Linda gave a quick glance over at Mary. Mary grabbed Rick's hand and led him away from where Linda and Susan were standing.

"Us girls had a long talk on the way up here and..."

Rick interrupted, "That is what I heard."

Mary sort of ignored his comment.

"And we decided that you and I are adults, and it is silly for three of us to be crammed into one room together, and since you have a room all by yourself, and..." Mary was struggling with her words now... "and we have spent the night in a tent together, you know." Rick knew where Mary was heading, so he helped her out.

"Would you like to just stay in my room, my sweet? It would be a lot less crowded."

Mary threw her arms around Rick's neck and gave him a kiss. "Whew, that was tough."

"You are so cute when your awkwardness comes out."

Mary broke her embrace and slapped Rick on the arm.

"You sure didn't help me out there."

"I had no idea where you were heading with everything," said Rick. "And if I had, I still would have let you stumble a little. You are so cute when you are shy."

Rick got another hit.

Linda and Susan were now passing by Rick and Mary. Linda just looked over at the two of them and gave a quick wink and a friendly smile.

"Linda and Susan said that it would be our little secret."

"I do like that lady," said Rick.

"They are both very nice ladies."

"They are a couple, aren't they?" Rick whispered when they were across the lobby.

"How did you know that?"

"I just have a good sense about these things." Plus, I remember when I was little, I had an Aunt Lillian. She was one classy dame, like Linda. She had a friend that we just called "other Aunt Lillian." I never did know her real name. They supposedly were just neighbors, but they were always together in Aunt Lillian's apartment. When I got older and a man of the world at thirteen, I figured it all out."

"That had to be worse for them back then," said Mary. "We talked about that a lot on the way up. They also have to be a little careful here in the South."

"I guess that will be our little secret on them, won't it," added Rick. "All these secrets, I hope I can keep them all straight."

"You will do better than me, I am sure."

Rick tossed his old Army duffle over his shoulder and reached down and picked up Mary's bag. They walked across the vast lobby towards the spaceship pods. They were all traveling up and down in a seemingly random pattern on their columns.

Mary and Rick got on one of the elevators and headed up. They moved very quickly, not giving time to contemplate whether it was a good idea or not. Once moving, however, the hypnotics view of the ground moving away so fast, and the massive walls of the hotel streaming past so quickly, left you with just a wow.

Mary and Rick dinged at the 16th floor and walked out of the elevator with the panoramic view of the hotel's grandeur below them. They approached the edge of the overhang, laced with the masses amount of green ivy covering the ledge.

"This is pretty cool," said Mary, as she leaned way over the plants and looked down over the ledge.

"Wish I could spit," she said.

"You are one sweet country girl," Rick said. "That's why I love you." Rick had meant it as just a figure of speech. Or did he? He did not have time to think about it.

As Mary turned to Rick, he knew she heard what he said, and she tossed her hands around his neck and gave him a big kiss over the ivy vines.

They made it to Rick's room. It was a lovely room with a fantastic view. In the far distance, off to the east was Stone Mountain, rising over all the Atlanta buildings and houses.

"This is great," said Mary, as she sat on the double bed with a couple big bounces.

Rick grabbed Mary by the hand and led her over to the large sliding glass door. They walked out onto the balcony. The city's noise below billowed upward, but the view and them being together overpowered it all.

Rick released Mary's hand and put his arm around her waist.

"It is so nice that you could come, Mary. I missed you," Rick said, as he squeezed her tighter.

"I did miss you, also."

They turned and did a long, passionate kiss.

After a seemingly long time on the balcony, Mary said, "Would it be ok if I take a quick shower, the dirt of the road, you know?"

"No problem, said Rick, breaking from their embrace. "I made reservations for dinner at the rotating restaurant at the top of this place in a couple of hours. I thought we could go up early and make one revolution over drinks.

"One revolution?" Said Mary.

"Yes, the whole place turns one revolution every 45 minutes, so you can see a view of Atlanta."

"That sounds amazing," said Mary, "Not real but amazing."

Mary took a shower, and they both changed into some more appropriate evening clothes.

The elevator for the Polaris was a short walk from their room. It was the center elevator that was designated just for the bar/restaurant on the roof.

A narrow table extended around the outside of the circular perimeter of the dome. All the chairs faced outward towards the city.

Rick and Mary sat at two of these chairs, nursing a few glasses of wine for the 45-minute trip around.

They then had a wonderful dinner of beef tenderloin that they asked to split into two portions. This was reluctantly but happily done by the staff. Rick was good at joking and respecting people that were waiting on him. They all related and realized that he and Mary were their kind of people instead of the high rolling people that they were used to at this place. They all laughed and had a good time together. It was a most excellent meal and evening. More importantly, Mary was having the evening of her life. Watching Rick laugh and make others laugh was making her fall in love with him that much more.

By the time they got out of the dome, it was nine o'clock.

On the way out to the elevator, Rick asked, "I thought we could go to the Underground and do some dancing, but it is getting kind of late. What do you think?"

"That is a nice thought, Rick, but I am pretty beat. It has been a very long day and a soft bed and a good night's sleep sounds really good."

"I hear you, girl," I was running a mile at 0600-hours this morning."

They went back to the room, where they both went their separate ways to get ready for bed. As much as they had come to know each other, both Rick and Mary were still on the shy side. Mary changed into the usual long nightshirt that she always wore and Rick into the boxer shorts he wore out of respect. Rick turned the light out, and they both slithered under

148

the soft white hotel sheets from opposite sides of the bed. They both stayed motionless on their backs, next to each other, facing the ceiling.

"So glad to be with you here, Rick," Mary said.

"And I with you, Mary, pretty darn nice, isn't it?"

They both turned and faced each other and shared a long and passionate kiss. Their two bodies could not get any closer together. The warmth and hardness of each of them were coming through their night ware. Mary stopped in the middle of their passionate kiss, sat up in bed, and removed her nightshirt.

"There, that is better," she said. "You might try the same, soldier boy."

Rick obeyed.

Rick and Mary were now lying down, facing each other, flesh on flesh. Feeling as close as they ever had, even more so than the tent of the week before. The kissing and the passion became a wild and crazy eruption of love and desire.

Again, they kept the promise to Mary's mother, but they satisfied each other to the fullest with hands, mouths, and fingers.

Rick woke first in the morning. Rick was lying on his back with Mary's head on his bare chest. Her long brown hair was flowing off to the side like a delicate woven shawl. Rick thought how very nice it was. He carefully lifted her head to one side and placed her softly on the pillow. Rick got out of bed, put his boxers on, and walked over to the glass doors and out on the balcony to watch the rising sun. He loved this peaceful time of day, and it was his favorite time to just appreciate life. The sun would rise right over Stone Mountain, the highest point in all directions. Just as the sun started peeking up over the horizon, Rick felt a sharp jab of a beautiful naked body across his back. He turned, and there was Mary with just a sheet on, wrapped around her like a Roman toga. Her nakedness in the front was a welcome sight to see as an early morning treat. They did a good morning kiss with a beautiful flesh-on-flesh hug. They turned again and stood side by side, arms

149

around each other, watching the sun come up over the horizon, and then over the top of Stone Mountain.

"A pretty nice way to start the day, don't you think," said Rick as he brought Mary closer to him.

"Yes, it is," said Mary as she looked up at Rick without him seeing her doing so. He was still watching the sunrise.

She was thinking, *God, I really am loving this man.*

Rick turned from the rising sun and caught Mary looking, and they did another nice kiss.

"How about some breakfast?" Rick said. "There is a place that is just a short walk away, and they have the best Biscuits and Gravy. A little ma and pa place."

After a short hesitation, Rick added, "Not as good as your uncle's diner's biscuits and gravy, of course."

"You better have added that, mister."

They got dressed and took the elevator pods down to the lobby.

The lobby was starting to get crowded as people were checking in. Rick had heard that there was some type of convention going on, American Legion, or something like that. From the looks of the crowds, it appeared there were going to be a lot of old folks, which was probably why the band was playing that night. They walked through the lobby towards the street tunnel. It became very apparent that they were the youngest people in the place. This was fine with Rick as he had found that old folks make the best audience for a swing band.

The breakfast place was only a few blocks walk. It was a small diner, not unlike Mary's uncles. They had an excellent breakfast and made plans for the day.

Rick had to be at a rehearsal with just the singers at 1000-hours in the ballroom. Mary had decided that she would just go along and watch.

They arrived at the ballroom a little before ten, so they had a chance to walk around the room.

It was A very large room that was fully carpeted except for a large hardwood dance floor in front of the stage. Tables were already set up over the carpeted area. Each had a centerpiece of flowers. The decorations were very patriotic, with a lot of American flags and banners. The ceiling was high, shaped in twenty-foot individual squares. In the center of each square was a six-foot square of crystal lighting. The crystal was layered with three tiers of glass extending down towards the carpeted floor. Everything followed the square theme.

A lovely place and a far cry from the Lake City warehouse. Rick felt a little scared at the thought of singing in a fancy place like this.

Mary noticed that Linda and Susan were sitting by the stage table, so she dragged Rick over to see them.

"Hey, you two," Linda said as they approached. "You guys are looking cute as ever, a couple right out of a Hollywood glamour magazine."

Rick and Mary were both a little embarrassed but took the compliment well.

"Did you two sleep well?" Rick said out of not knowing what else to say.

"We did great. The beds here are not like your normal hotel beds. And you two?"

Rick knew he opened himself up for that one, and both Linda and Susan were smiling, waiting for an answer.

"Good," was all Mary said.

"Ok, Rick, let's go see if anyone else is here," said Linda. "What are you two girls going to do?"

"I was just going to hang out here and wait around for Rick. How about you, Susan?"

"How about we just hang out together? I hear they won't be very long," said Susan.

When Rick and Linda arrived backstage, everyone was already there. Barb, Cathy, and Carol were all in one group while Ron and

151

Bob were off to the side. Everyone was already looking at their sheet music while Phil, the conductor, walked between the groups. Rick went around to each group and did warm handshakes with the guys and warm hugs with the ladies.

"Ok, here you go, Ricky boy," Bob brought over a pile of sheet music and handed it to Rick as Ron followed.

"We are pretty much doing the same things we did down in Lake City," Ron said. "Linda and I will still be doing the leads on everything. As you can see, the same songs. "One change, however, remember when the band did *Pennsylvania 65,000* and the band all shouted out? Well, Phil wants us all to do the same thing over the mics. It was weak from the band last time, and it might be weaker yet in this big place.

"That sounds easy enough," said Rick. "Anything else?"

Well, Phil just hit us with a couple of more changes. First, he wants to add *Indian Summer* as a vocal, but I will do it solo, so you guys will not have to worry.

"The other thing," Ron continued. "Have you ever done *I've Got a Gal in Kalamazoo*? I know we never have as a group."

"We all know what it is," said Carol. "It is not an easy one, I know that, especially for the backup singers."

"Can we do it?" Ron asked. "We will have the music in front of us."

"Of course, we can do it, but it will take some practice," said Barb.

"What about you, Rick?" Asked Ron.

"I am from Michigan, you know. That was one of the most requested songs by the old folks up there. It is a tricky one, as I remember. Thank God we can have sheet music."

"Ok, let's do it." Ron said. "I think we better start with it.

Everyone got together in a small semicircle with sheet music in hand.

"Ready," Ron said. As he started.

A-B-C-D-E-F-G-H.   I got a gal (in Kalamazoo).....

152

Phil came over from time to time and sat down in a chair facing the group, just looking up at the ceiling and listening. He frowned a couple of times but most of the time just nodded his head in agreement. Afterward, he gave some critiques but mostly a series of compliments.

They were finished at around noon.

"Good to have you on board again, Rick," Bob said as they left the backstage area. "Nice to have some young blood in this old group. And I brought you a tux that will fit you this time."

"I am so glad you asked me to come back, I love it, and you people are so much fun to be around."

Rick walked out of the backstage area and across the stage. The hotel people were already setting up the bandstand seats and front panels on stage. It looked like the band had spruced up things a lot since Lake City. Rick finally made his way through the chaos and to Mary's table.

"Can I steal this lady from you now?" Rick said as he grabbed Mary by the hand. Mary turned quickly to Susan as she was dragged away and said, "It was nice talking with you. See you later at rehearsal!"

Rick walked Mary across the carpet to the stairs.

"Sounds good, girl," came Susan's voice, fading into the distance.

At the top of the stairs, still holding hands, Rick turned Mary towards him, and they shared a friendly kiss.

"Did you miss me?" said Rick.

"Of course, but I did have a nice talk with Susan. She is a very nice lady, but do I have some news."

"Ok," Rick said, "But you can tell me over lunch as I want to hurry and take you to the Atlanta Underground before I have to get back here at 4 o'clock."

They walked to the Underground as it was only a few blocks from the Hyatt.

The Underground was relatively new, like the Hyatt Regency.

Rick and Mary walked up and down the old streets that were the basements of old buildings built after Atlanta was destroyed during the Civil War. It was laced with history but also contained many shops, bars, and restaurants. It would have been nice to spend some time looking at the old buildings, but Rick had to be back in only a few hours. They did stop at former Governor Lester Maddox's Restaurant and souvenir shop and split a catfish sandwich. Out of curiosity more than anything. The catfish was delicious, and the ax handles and other memorabilia were very different. Unexpectedly, Lester Maddox personally sat down at Rick and Mary's table and talked with them for a very long time and gave them a free ice-cream dessert. He said he was glad to see young people, like them, in his place.

As they left the restaurant, Mary whispered, "Well, that was interesting. Who'd a thought."

"I know," said Rick. "Lester Maddox himself."

"He actually was a very nice man," said Mary.

"Yes, he was. He did raise some hell during the civil rights movement with his old restaurant, however."

"Yes, I read he was definitely a segregationist."

"He always denied he was a segregationist, only that people should be able to decide for themselves."

"I did read that the black leaders in the state did say after his death that he did more for the black people of Georgia than any other governor."

"All that is so complicated," said Mary. "Who knows what is true."

"Well, you can now impress all your friends by telling them that you had lunch with Lester Maddox while you were in Atlanta."

"That will probably go over big."

154

"I bet your dad will be impressed."

"You're probably right on that one."

Rick and Mary got back to the Hyatt just before four o'clock, so they went right down to the ballroom. The place was much different than when they had left. The room was now full of people. Rick figured many of those sitting at tables were just friends of band members and other curious guests from the hotel. The stage was now full of musicians. Some were tuning, polishing, and caressing their instruments. Others were fluffing up sheet music on their music stands. Phil, the conductor, was weaving in and out of the seats, just looking around and talking with everyone. Linda and the whole singing crew were off to the right of the band members. Mary spotted Susan sitting alone at a table off to the side, so they went over to say hi. Susan saw them coming and stood up.

"Hey, you two," she said. "Nice to see some familiar faces. I was getting pretty bored sitting here."

Mary let go of Rick's hand and rushed over to sit down on the chair next to Susan.

"We just hiked over to the Underground. Have you been there?" Mary asked.

"No, I haven't," said Susan.

"Maybe we should walk over there while our people here are rehearsing," Mary said. "Would that be ok with you, Rick?"

"Of course, it would. I was hoping you two would do something instead of just sitting here."

"Great," Mary said as she got up from her chair and gave Rick a friendly kiss.

"I better get up on stage before I get fired. You two have fun. How about we just meet back in the room? You don't have to rush."

Rick headed to the stage and joined the other singers.

Linda was the first to come out of the group and approach Rick, "Hey, sweetie, how are you doing?"

"Great, we just got back from the Underground," Rick said. "In fact, our ladies have gone off to the Underground to play." *Crap,* Rick thought, I *just referred to Susan as her lady.* Linda thought nothing of it, fortunately.

"Here we go, Rick. Are you ready to play it again Sam," Linda said as she grabbed Rick's hand, and they joined the other singers at their mics.

It was a full practice that went on for a couple of hours. The band played shortened versions of all the numbers they would play that evening, and the singers did the same. Rick had been worried about the *Kalamazoo* thing, but they pulled it off wonderfully. It all went smoothly, and he felt so much better about things then he had in Lake City when he had to go-in-cold. He was feeling great but very tired, and his throat hurt.

Rick went up to the room carrying the tux that Bob had brought for him. Mary had not gotten back yet, so Rick took a quick shower and dropped down for a short nap.

He was still sleeping when Mary got back up to the room.

Quietly crawling next to Rick, she kissed him on the cheek. As Rick slowly opened his eyes, he saw Mary looking at him.

"Are you the one who called room service for an escort for this evening?" Mary whispered loudly.

"That had to be me. I hope you're not too expensive as my girlfriend just spent all my money shopping," Rick said as he looked over at the bags Mary had brought in with her.

"I am sure we can work something out. I do have a discount rate for soldiers."

They did a lengthy kiss.

"You had probably better get going. You do have to be down in the ballroom in 20 minutes, you know."

"Holy shit," Rick said. "I didn't realize how late it was. Good thing you came when you did."

Rick jumped up and was in his tux, kissed Mary goodbye, and headed out the door in five minutes.

"See you down there later, sweetly," he said as he left the room.

By the time Rick got to the ballroom, the tables in the room had already started to fill. The band members were already in their seats. Rick went backstage to join the rest of the singers. Bob was the first to approach Rick.

"Looking good there, buddy," he said as he snuck his flask out of his pocket and handed it to Rick. "I knew you were going to need a little of this."

"Thanks, you know me already, don't you," Rick said as he took a couple of big swigs from the flask.

From the first time Rick met Bob in Lake City, he knew that they had some type of bond going. They just seemed to like each other right away. Maybe it was because he was also single or Rick was closer to his age than any of the other guys. He was probably in his late forties. Or it might have been that Rick loved sharing his flask. Whatever it was, Rick appreciated the camaraderie of it all and how Bob make him feel welcome in the group.

"Ok, boys and girls, let's get out there and go nuts," said Linda as she led the way to their microphones on stage.

The ballroom was now packed.

Where Rick was standing on his corner of the stage, he could see Mary coming across the dance floor to a small table where Susan was sitting. She was looking as beautiful as ever, with a baby blue evening gown that was opened nicely at the front. The laced white shawl over her shoulders amplified the beauty of her long brown hair. "God, I do love that lady," Rick mumbled to himself. "Get a grip buddy, you have to concentrate here."

The band, of course, started off with *In the Mood*.

The first song for the singers was *Tuxedo Junction*, followed by Rick and Bob helping Linda and Ron with *Well All Right*.

Phil had set the Kalamazoo song to come after Ron did *Indian Summer*. If it was a flop, *Indian Summer* would be fresh in their minds.

They pulled it off wonderfully. Rick was amazed at how well it came together.

"You people are amazing," Rick said to everyone as they left the stage for the break. "That was pretty cool."

"You did great yourself, young man," said Cathy.

"We have about a 20-minute break here, Rick," said Linda, "if you want to go out and say hi to Mary."

"Thanks," answered Rick. "That would be nice."

Rick went out onto the ballroom floor and over to Mary and Susan's table. Mary had ordered Rick a glass of scotch on the rocks, so it was waiting for him.

"You are so sweet," Rick said. "You knew I would need this, didn't you?"

He gave Mary a nice kiss.

"So, what did you think?"

"This wine is wonderful," Mary said.

After a long pause, she continued, "Oh, you mean how were you up there. Silly me. You and everybody sounded marvelous, really."

"I am glad because it is so much fun up there," answered Rick.

Recorded music started playing loudly over the ballroom's speaker system.

"Would you like to dance, my dear?" said Rick.

"I would love to, kind sir."

They walked out onto the dance floor and snuggled in close together, moving to a lovely slow song. They were both enjoying the movement of their warm bodies touching.

"You are a very nice dancer," Mary said.

"You are pretty good yourself, young lady. I did notice you and Susan were getting some good practice on the dance floor with a few of these old farts in here."

"Yes, I know. I think we made those gentlemen's evening."

"You did for sure, as you are the nicest looking lady in the place."

"And don't forget, probably the youngest," Mary said.

"That too," said Rick.

Mary just smiled and put her head back on Rick's shoulder, and they danced.

They only got a couple of good dances in before Rick had to get back on stage. Those two dances were interrupted constantly with old folks wanting to tell Rick what an excellent job he and the band were doing.

The dancing with Mary ended way too soon, when Rick at to leave.

The second set with the band went very quickly, and before Rick realized it, they were finished.

When the concert was over, and everyone gave their final bows, Phil came over to all the singers and praised everyone for doing a fine job.

"I was a little concerned about Kalamazoo," he said. "But you people pulled it off wonderfully, like always."

He singled out Rick and shook his hand.

"And thank you, young man, for joining us again. You are welcome anytime."

"I might take you up on that, sir. I thoroughly enjoyed every minute of it."

Mary and Susan were waiting at the edge of the stage when Rick hopped down and gave Mary a kiss and a hug.

"Hey, you two, a group of us are going up top to the Polaris Room to have a nightcap and watch the city lights go by. Want to come?" Linda said as she walked towards them.

Looking at Mary, Rick asked, "What do you think?"

"That sounds great," she said.

"Wonderful," said Linda as she went over to Susan and asked the same thing.

Rick and Mary went out into the lobby, where it was packed with people from the dance. The side elevators had lines but the center one to the roof did not, so they got on right away and headed to the rotating bar. The view from the glass elevators was exciting as usual, especially at night with the glow of the elevator's outside lights.

There were not many people in the bar, so Rick and Mary found a lovely table with seats facing out over the city. Rick ordered a Scotch and Mary a glass of red wine. Rick moved his chair around next to Mary's so they could sit next to each other.

"This is pretty nice," Mary said.

"Yes, it is," Rick said as he reached over and held Mary's hand.

"This whole weekend has been just wonderful," Mary said softly as she squeezed Rick's hand a little tighter. "It is going to be sad to leave you tomorrow."

"I know, but we have the rest of the night and tomorrow morning to be together, so let us not think about anything else."

Just then, a large, loud group stepped off the elevator and came stumbling toward Rick and Mary. It was, of course, band people, who obviously had already started drinking medicine. Linda and Susan, Barb, Cathy, and Carol. Ron was with his wife Julie, and of course, Bob. They all pulled up chairs around Rick and Mary's tiny table and started all the introductions. After everyone met Mary and the small talk was out of the way, the conversation went to the performance and the music. Everyone seemed to talk at once, but everything was understood by all. Rick could tell that Mary was loved, and they made her feel part of the group and conversation. He could also see that Mary was excited about these people and their passion for what they did. Bob made sure he sat on the other

160

side of Mary, where he was both charming and flirting at the same time. Mary loved the attention, and Rick was so proud of her for holding her own with him and fitting right in with everyone else. They all sat and talked and drank for one complete revolution of the dome, which took about 45 minutes. The city lights were a sight to see, and the laughs were terrific. The closeness and camaraderie with everyone were what Rick loved the best about these music people. Watching Mary interact and laugh with everyone made him love Mary that much more.

Starting the second revolution, Rick turned to Mary and said, "How about we leave these people and go find a quiet place?"

"That sounds like an excellent plan to me, like how about our room?"

"I like the way you think there, girl."

They said their goodnights to everyone and headed down to the lobby and back up to their 16th-floor room.

Rick kicked off his shoes and tossed his tux coat on a chair. Mary did the same with her shoes and threw her lace shawl on top of Rick's coat.

They both threw themselves, flat on their backs, on top of the newly made bed. Rick, still in his fancy tux, and Mary still in her lovely evening gown. They just remained motionless there for a few minutes, taking deep breaths.

"Now that was a full day," Rick said as he reached over and held Mary's outstretched hand.

"Yes, it was," Mary answered back. "We did cram a lot into it, didn't we?"

"Hope you enjoyed yourself, Mary, and you were not too bored."

"You are kidding me. I loved every minute of it. And the day is not over yet," Mary said as she lifted herself off her back and rolled over on top of Rick. She gave Rick a long and sensual kiss, then put her head next to his. They remained motionless for a long

161

moment just feeling each other's breath. Rick could feel the heat in between them rising.

Mary then softly whispered into Rick's ear. "You know I have been thinking about you all day long, and I have decided that..." Mary hesitated for a moment, then continued. "The deep love that we share for each other overrides a daughter's promise to her mother. What do you think?"

"A," Rick now was stumbling for words. "You are asking me a question like that while lying on top of me with your warm body. Looking as beautiful as you are. You know that is not a fair question."

Mary did not wait for Rick to say anything else. She just gave him the most passionate kiss that she had ever given another man. Rick kissed her back with an equal passion. Mary sat up, still on Rick's lap, and started unbuttoning his white tux shirt. She tore it open and started kissing Rick's chest.

Rick reached around Mary's back and was able to slide the zipper of that lovely blue dress all the way down her lower back. Mary got up quickly from lying on Rick's chest, and the front of her dress fell in front of her, piled at her waist. Exposing her lovely, gown-matching, blue bra. She slowly crawled off Rick and stepped to the bedside floor, where her gown dropped to the carpet. She gracefully stepped out of the dress, bent over, picked it up, and tossed it onto the chair. She stood there for a moment for Rick's benefit, showing off her blue bra and matching laced blue panties.

"So, what do you think, big boy," Mary said as she did a quick twirl around. "Do I know how to color coordinate or what?"

Rick had now set himself up on the side of the bed. He was not thinking about the fashion statement at that moment, only the beauty standing before him.

Mary grabbed Rick's hand and pulled him off the bed to stand in front of her. She unbuttoned the last few buttons on his

162

shirt and took it off over his shoulders and down his arms. Mary tossed it on top of her blue gown on the chair. She then went to Rick's tux pants and undid the buckle, unsnapped, and zipped down. The weight of the heavy belt sent the pants crashing to the ground at Rick's feet. Mary went down and lifted Rick's feet, one at a time, out of the pants. While she was there, she gently removed Rick's socks and tossed them with the pants.

Rick just stood there absorbing the reality of it all. Standing up and facing Rick, she looked into his eyes. As Rick looked back into hers, the smiles on their faces were broad. They did a long hard kiss, pushing their bodies as close as they could get. The passion was out, and there was no stopping it now. Rick unsnapped Mary's bra and tossed it to the carpet. He grabbed her blue laced panties, bent his knees, and followed them down to the floor, where they stayed. On his way up from lifting himself from the floor, Mary grappled his boxers and pulled them down as he went up. They were now facing each other in a harder than ever embrace and kiss. Still in an embrace, Rick led Mary back to the bed. With one hand, he turned down the bedspread, exposing white, clean sheets. With the other hand, he gently lowered Mary onto the sheets. They were now side by side, looking into each other's eyes.

"Are you sure about this?" asked Rick.

"Of course, I am, Dear." "I love you, and this feels so right to me."

"I love you, Mary."

They embraced side by side. Kissing now more passionately than they had ever before. Rick felt Mary's soft breasts against his bare chest. Her soft nipples were now becoming harder against his. Just when Rick thought he could not get more excited, Mary reached over and placed her warm hand around him. The passion and excitement raced through them at the same time.

Rick's lips left Mary's lips and traveled down to Mary's hardened nipples. His tongue and teeth gently massaged them till

163

they were like granite outcrops. Mary moaned a sigh of intense pleasure.

Her grip released him, and her fingers stroked the hair on the back of his head as he continued to excite her lovely breast.

He slowly kissed down her firm stomach. Sending kiss after kiss to her soft abdominal skin.

With both hands, he reached around her back and gently grabbed her rounded cheeks.

He continued kissing the warm flesh of her stomach down through the soft, fluffy jungle. He reached the essence of her forbidden womanhood. Here he again repeated a kiss after kiss of pure passion and a long tongue of joy.

Mary moaned with a delight of joy as she still stroked the hair on the back of his head. A stroke of not gentleness anymore but now of fierce passion and grabbing desire.

Rick slowly moved back up Mary's body till he reached her sweet lips again. They again shared a long and passionate kiss. The kiss lasted for simply an eternity. There was nothing to stop the passion now. They were going forward into a place where they both were explorers of new lands.

Rick lowered himself with more weight on top of Mary. His hardness was now at full potential. Mary grabbed him and forced him into her.

Mary's wetness was so extreme that it was dripping onto the sheets. Mary was small, and Rick was significant, but the dampness made it an easy fit.

They paused for a moment, looking at each other again. Rick and Mary's eyes meeting gave a look of love and a passion. A love and affection that was so immense and so longing that there was no turning back now.

"I love you, Mary."

"And I do love you so much, Rick."

The rhythm started.

The motion of love and passion went on and on.

Until the satisfaction ended in one giant blast for both. Silence overwhelmed the room.

They just held tight their embrace, inside one another.

Love was glowing so intently that it left them speechless. A warmth surrounded them that only could be described from a fairytale.

All of Rick and Mary's searching for treasures in nature. In the swamps, above and below the water. What they were looking for was there all the time between them. Nature, the treasures, the adventures, was just this. The love and passion between them were better than any explorer could ever wish for.

"I do love you, Girl."

"And I you, Rick."

They fell asleep in each other's arms.

The bright Georgia sun came shining through the east-facing window that Rick loved so much. He or Mary were not up to watch it this morning. They were both still deep in sleep and glowing from the night before.

Rick was barely awake but still felt Mary's warm breath on his face and her perky breasts pressing against his lower chest.

Mary twisted her legs to get closer to Rick, causing Rick's morning hardness to poke her into her soft stomach.

"Oh," said Mary. "I guess all of you is awake now, isn't it?"

They both laughed. Mary then reached down and grabbed Rick's hardness and stroked it just enough to bring out a calming sigh from Rick.

Mary then let go and tossed off the sheet that was covering them. She flung her leg over Rick's body and sat upright on his hips. She lowered her naked body down on his and gave him a wild and passionate kiss. Sitting back up, she once again grabbed onto Rick's hardness and forced it into her. Her passion and excitement had caused her wetness to flow again. No force was

165

needed. Rick and Mary both sighed simultaneously, except Rick came out with an "oh my."

Mary, still sitting upright, started moving with a gentle and complex rhythm at the same time. Rick just froze there, not being able to move but wanting to. Mary was doing all the work. Rick felt himself deep inside her, and Mary felt him there as well. Mary was still sitting, but Rick was now allowed to move. They both started moving in a perfectly synchronized motion like they were the same person. Moving gently, passionately, slowly, slowly. The frequency increased. Slow to fast...then faster. Mary came down on Rick and looked into his eyes with such a loving and passionate look that it made Rick give up all. In one giant surge. Mary followed immediately with the same surge. She collapsed onto Rick's body. Both were still moving in the same rhythm but much slower. Still connected, they shared another long and passionate kiss.

"Good morning, Mr. Rick."

"A very good morning to you, and I mean a really good morning," Rick answered back.

"Yes, it was a very good morning," said Mary. "Not a bad way to start the day is it."

"Not bad at all."

They held tight onto one another for a very long time, just enjoying each other's warmth and love.

"I do not want this weekend to end," said Mary.

"Me neither," said Rick. "It has been so great being here and sharing everything with you."

"And I bet you mean, everything, don't you?"

"Yes, everything, The band, the music, new friends, the Hyatt, Atlanta, everything."

"Is that it?" Mary asked.

"Yes, I think that is about it," said Rick.

"You are such a jerk," Mary said as she lifted one hand to slap Rick.

Rick caught it in mid-air and pulled Mary close with it.

"I guess I did leave something out, didn't I?"

He kissed Mary long and hard.

"Ok," Rick said as he forced his way out of Mary's arms, "we need to get moving here. I'm going to splurge and get us a room service breakfast."

"That would be very sweet."

"Why don't you go take a shower, and I will call and order. How about eggs Benedict? Bet you don't serve that at your uncle's diner."

"No, we don't, and I am not sure I have ever had it," said Mary.

"Well, you're in for a treat."

"I have a better idea," said Mary. "Why don't you go order breakfast and come and join me in the shower."

"That is a better idea. You are such a little hussy."

That got Rick a good slap on the arm.

"Maybe I am, but you love it."

"Yes, I do."

Rick ordered breakfast and joined Mary in the shower.

They washed each other's backs.

They sat at a tiny little table on the balcony, clothed in only the Hyatt Regency white bathrobes, and enjoyed their breakfast. It was a warm southern morning which was an indicator that the day would be a hot one.

Mary was right. She had never had eggs Benedict, before, but she was surely going to have them again. She was impressed.

They got dressed and packed, as checkout time was closing in very fast. Rick and Mary met Linda and Susan in the lobby.

Linda perked up when she saw Rick and Mary approaching.

"Good morning, you two. Did you sleep well?" Linda said as she gave both Rick and Mary a hug. "You both have a big grin on your faces, so it must have been a good night."

Rick and Mary did not quite know what she met by that, but both their faces warmed up. The look on Linda's face showed that she meant exactly what Rick and Mary thought she meant. Their faces got warmer yet. Susan was wisely staying out of the conversation.

They all walked out to the parking lot together. Rick walked Mary to Linda's car. Linda and Susan got in right away, but Mary stayed out with Rick by the trunk.

Holding each other close.

"Thank you for a wonderful weekend," Mary said.

"No, thank you, I am so glad you could share it with me."

They did a kiss.

"Is it ok to come and visit you next weekend?" Rick asked.

"You had better, mister."

"I get Fridays off for PT, so we need to do something physical."

"What I have in mind I don't think you can put in your report, soldier," Mary said as she pulled Rick in closer.

"You do know that I am going to miss you terribly, don't you," said Mary.

"I will be missing you also," said Rick as he drew Mary closer yet and they shared a very long kiss goodbye.

"I love you."

"I love you."

As Mary was getting into the car, she yelled back,

"Bring your SCUBA gear. I have another surprise for you."

"Will do."

Rick tossed his duffle into his Jeep and was off for Augusta. A two-hour drive that was certainly going to be filled with some heavy thinking. He was going off to play soldier once again. Once again, but not for too much longer. He was missing Mary already, but the thought that he was finally going to be out of the Army was overriding the sadness of missing Mary.

CHAPTER 11
Ted and the Climb

When Rick first met Ted, they were waiting for orders to ship out for Vietnam. They were both Signal Corp. Ted was a first lieutenant because he did ROTC in college, and Rick was a repair and maintenance instructor. They became good friends as they shared the same adventure interests and goals. Ted was from Montana, and although he lived in the city of Bozeman, he had that cowboy look. He had that image of being tall and lanky, but he was the same height as Rick. Ted had light brown hair with a long face. He spoke slow like a Montana cowboy, but he also laughed hard like one. Ted was an avid mountain climber and diver. He had stories, like Rick. Rick had never climbed, so Ted had promised to teach him the-ropes'. It ended up that Rick got orders for Nam and Ted went to Germany. That was a good thing for Ted as first lieutenants did not fare well in Nam. The first lieutenant butter-bar on their helmets stood out to Charlie Cong as an excellent target as they knew it marked an officer. The mortality rate was right up there with door gunners, for obvious reasons, and radio operators with their antennae coming out of their backpacks. The first lieutenants learned early to use black shoe polish on their bars to cover them up. The poor door gunners did not have an out, other than fire as many rounds as they could. Radio operators less options. Ted returned from Germany the same time Rick came back from Nam. They were both short-timers, so they were able to indulge in many of their adventures together before their discharge.

Sitting in the Officers Mess Hall over a cup of coffee, Ted said, "We need to get some climbing in soon before it gets too hot down here. Most of the rock outcrops that I climb are south facing, and they get boiling during the day."

"Anytime, buddy," said Rick.

That was all it took, and Rick was a little shocked when they were suddenly heading towards Atlanta the following weekend. It was mid-May, so not yet extremely hot. They headed north of Atlanta towards Tennessee and the Chattanooga area. After they went through Chattanooga, Rick stopped his Jeep and let Ted drive as he knew where he was going. He was glad he did, as they made many turns on a lot of obscure roads. The last could not even be called a road. It was more a lane: two ruts, with thick grass growing in the center. This lane, it seemed, went on for miles. They went uphill and downhill through heavily forested areas. They finally came to a large clearing where the rutted lane ended.

"Here we are," said Ted.

"And where are we exactly," said Rick. "I hope you don't fall off a cliff here, as I will never find my way back to anywhere."

"Secret spots are never easy to find, you know, otherwise they would not stay secret."

"It is stunning and wild around here," Rick said.

They unloaded all the climbing gear and placed it into backpacks with water and food for lunch. They started hiking up a narrow path that was surrounded by overhanging vegetation on both sides. There were so many trees blocking the sun, it seemed like dusk rather than the middle of the day. They walked about a half-mile and came to a large clearing in the forest. In front of them was a large rock outcrop that was at least fifty feet wide and extended straight upward to where it went out of sight above the trees. As they approached the giant monolith, Rick started to get a little anxious and scared as to what he had agreed to.

This was his first-ever climbing adventure. Ted was going to guide him through the basics. Rick had gone through Airborne training and had many jumps under his belt but climbing up the side of a chunk of rock was seeming to be a little more than he was ready for. As the rock outcrop started getting larger and closer, he wondered whether it was a good idea.

They got to the base of the rock at about noon. It was hot, even in the shade of all the trees. Ted was right as it was a south-facing rock face and later in the summer would be very hot to touch. It was at least 100 feet high. It was small compared to the Rocky Mountains that Rick had skied many times, but this looked very high as it was framed by the trees and was large compared to the surrounding mountains. The face of the rock was at least not straight up like Rick had feared. It started out very gradual and towards the top looked a little steeper, but not like the wall that Rick had visioned.

They unloaded their packs, and Ted started hauling out the climbing equipment. As they unpacked, Ted began giving Rick some basic lessons in climbing.

"Now, this is a pretty easy climb," Ted said. "It is not real steep but is a gradual slope until right at the top, where it will be more vertical. There are, however, plenty of ledges and cracks to hang onto and place your feet in. Reality and fear took over for Rick, and Ted could tell by the expression on Rick's face.

"Are you sure you are up for this?" asked Ted.

Rick snapped out of his fear mode as what little macho image he had was about to go down the toilet.

Rick said, out loud and a little to himself, "Come on, you dummy, you have walked steel on narrow little I-beams with no safety line, jumped out of airplanes. Come on, how hard can this be."

171

Ted tossed Rick a climbing harness.

"Here you go, try this on,"

Rick played with it for a minute before he asked,

"Ok, I give up. I have no clue which body part goes where."

Ted was enjoying watching Rick struggling.

"I guess you need a lesson, don't you?"

"I guess I do," said Rick.

Ted took the harness from Rick and untangled the mess that Rick had managed. He held it in front of Rick.

"Here, just put your legs in these two openings like you are putting on a pair of underwear."

Ted showed Rick how to tighten the leg straps and the safe way to loop the belt buckle. Ted attached a locking carabiner to the front belt loop and screwed down the locking screw. He tied Rick's climbing rope with a double figure-eight knot.

"There you go. You are now a mountain climber. I probably should have given you more training, but with all the shit we have been through in the Army, and we know how much training they gave us."

"The main thing for me is if I slip, you can catch me or at least slow me down. This is called a figure-eight. It supplies friction to my rope if I start to fall. You just must never let go of this rope right here, no matter what. If I fall, your weight will be pulled up, and I can land nicely at the last anchor.

I have anchors in from my last trip here, and I will just check them on the way up to make sure they are good.

I will take your rope up with me and top anchor you, and then you can follow in my footsteps, sort of speak. Just do exactly what I do, and you will be good. If you fall, I will stop your fall from the top. Any questions?"

"Yeah, right," Rick said. "You have to be kidding me."

"You'll do fine."

Before Rick could say any more, Ted was already scrambling up the loose rocks at the base.

The next thing Rick knew, Ted was halfway up the face, threading his rope through the anchors as he went. Rick's adrenaline was flowing so much that it seemed like a very short time, when he saw Ted's leg disappear over the rim of rock at the top. The last he saw was the bottom of his shoes go past the bright red rope that Rick was dangling on. Rick worked his way towards the top, trying to remember where Ted had placed his hand and feet. Ted had gone so far ahead that it was becoming difficult to follow his exact route. Fortunately, Rick had the rope and anchors to follow. Looking up, he saw just Ted's face grinning over the side of the rock.

"Hey, are you coming or not?"

Ted had carried Rick's rope up with him and tied off at the top, so Ted would do a top belay for him. Rick left Ted's rope, tied his rope off to his harness, and started scrambling to the steep section. When he got to the steep cliff, he just took a deep breath and started slowly moving up, one foot or hand at a time.

Rick kept concentrating so hard on where to put his next foot and handhold that before he knew it, he was almost to the top. Slowly he worked his way to the overhanging ledge. Rick pulled himself over the top. He was so glad he had Ted's rope to pull himself up with.

As soon as Rick was safely over the ledge, Ted dropped Rick's safety rope, sat down on a rock, and drank from his flask.

Rick crawled over to Ted and sat down beside him. Ted handed him the flask.

"Here you go, buddy. You deserve a good belt."

Rick took a sip. It was straight Jack Daniels, and it tasted wonderful. Rick could not believe that Ted brought it all the way up the rock.

The view was amazing. The rock they were on stood out above the treetops in an otherwise unbroken field of green trees. Occasionally a rock outcrop would be protruding out of the trees off in the distance. They were on an island in the middle of a green ocean. It was wonderful. Rick was dead tired, worn out, his hand and feet were sore, but now it all seemed somehow so worth it.

He felt great and alive. It was always hard to explain to others the feeling of accomplishment. Overcoming an obstacle of nature. Or maybe risking death to some extent that made you feel alive. Something he learned from reading Hemingway. It was a nice feeling of being alive. It was great to appreciating life, the mountain, himself, and being away from the Army. Getting out of the Army soon. It all was good. He had been close to death a few times, especially over the past three years and the feeling was always the same. Too bad you must be forced into those extremes to feel life that way.

"Well, buddy, what do you think about this climbing shit?" Asked Ted.

"Not bad," Rick said. "I wish you would have taken me for the first time, maybe on a ten-foot piece of rock instead of a 100-foot chunk of crumbly granite. You were a good teacher and guide, buddy. Thanks, it was a good one."

"It was not the proper, safe way to learn to climb, especially for you belaying me, but we did it," said Ted.

They drank up the rest of the flask of JD.

They hung out at the top of the rock for a long while, then Ted gave Rick a quick lesson in rappelling down with his figure-eight.

"Ok," Rick said, "that seems pretty easy." He did not mean what he said but did not want to tell Ted what he thought.

"You go first, as I have to pick up our anchors and rope as I go down."

Rick lowered himself over the side of the rock until he came to the first anchor. He was scared shitless as the 100-foot drop looked a lot farther down now, and he had no idea what he was doing. How he wished he had practiced off a bunk or something. Rick slowly fed the rope through the figure-eight and found himself slowly descending to the waiting ground below. Not as bad as he thought, but he still was scared shitless. It seemed to take forever as he moved slowly to the ground. He reached the base of the outcrop and wanted to kiss the ground but did not want to blemish his macho image in front of Ted again. Rick looked up at Ted and watched him quickly hop over the edge and descend to the first anchor. He disconnected his rope and fell very fast to the next one. Rick was impressed as it did look like Ted knew what he was doing and was so comfortable at it. Rick knew he was showing off a little of his skill to impress him, and he did. He was down in no time, smiling another big grin.

"Now that was a climb," Ted said. "Thanks for sharing it with me. It is hard to find anyone that will."

"Hey, it was a real trip, and I loved it now that it is over. Thanks for teaching me the ropes, buddy."

"No problem, you're an easy student."

"I will pay you back someday," said Rick.

"I am counting on it."

Rick and Ted loaded the climbing gear into the Jeep, had a little lunch, and headed back towards Atlanta. Rick drove now. As much as he liked and trusted Ted, he did not like other people driving his Jeep. They had planned to get a motel somewhere in Atlanta but decided to do a marathon, and just head back to Augusta.

It was a great climbing trip, and Ted and Rick had formed a stronger bond because of it. Once a bond is established between guys over an adventure, it can never be broken. It is forever.

CHAPTER 12
Devil's Ear

It was a slow week on post for Rick. Quiet but good as there were no surprises like guard duty or bus driving. He led the regular PT classes at 0600-hours and taught lessons the rest of the day. He did have supper with Ted in the Officer's Club one night. They talked about their rock climb.

"That was a fun one for sure," said Rick

"We need to do it again when the weather gets cooler," said Ted.

"A, Sir, need I remind you that I am a short-timer around here, and I will be out of this man's Army in a month.

"Oh, how could I forget that" Ted said. "Probably because you are an asshole. I do have another six months left; you know."

"Sorry about that, but the price you pay for being a Jar-Head."

"Have you thought about what you'll be doing yet?" Ted asked in a little more serious tone.

"I have no idea, other than whatever I want to. I thought about just cruising the country and mooching off old Army buddies for places to stay."

"Well, if you're ever in Montana, be sure and look me up. We have some good climbing up there."

"I will for sure, buddy."

Rick paused, "There is Mary. I really love this lady, but between my newfound freedom and her going away to school, I don't see how this will have a happy ending."

"That is always a tough one," said Ted. "A day at a time, soldier. That's what got you through Nam and us through this damn Army, you know."

"That is how I am trying to handle it all. Mary is such a sweetie, though."

Ted ordered another round of drinks.

"Not to change the subject," Ted said, but I have been thinking lately about your invite to try some cave diving. Are you still up for doing that before you leave?"

"That would be great. Actually, I have been thinking the same thing after visiting all those springs down in Florida with Mary."

"Your stories about those springs are what got me thinking about it also."

"It has been a while for me. I did a few caves with some college buddies when I went to school in Fort Meyers. We didn't go real deep into them but deep enough to get the feel of what it was like. It is pretty cool."

"Anytime is good for me," said Ted.

"Mary had said that her boyfriend in high school was a big cave diver and took her to a lot of springs around her hometown. She would love to show us some of them, I am sure. Mary is a great diver but said there was no way she would do a cave."

"She dives, huh? Sounds like my kind of woman already."

"Hey, she is taken."

"Actually, she did ask me if I knew any cute guys for her girlfriend, Sandy."

"Well, here I am."

"I said she wanted a cute guy."

"You are an asshole."

"How about I ask her this weekend? I would love for you to meet her, anyway."

"Sounds good to me," said Ted with subtle enthusiasm.

"How about in two weeks?" Rick said.

"You don't mess around. I guess that would work."

"I start processing out shortly after that, so there is a pretty small window."

"You're right. Processing out takes about a week."

"I don't see why they can't just say "bye'" and kick us out," answered Rick.

"I hear you, but it is the Army way. Make your life miserable till the very end."

"I'll drink to that," said Rick as he clinked Ted's glass of Scotch with his.

The rest of the week went by fast, and the next thing Rick knew, he had his Jeep loaded and was on the long drive to Mary's.

He did his usual in-town stop at the diner to let Mary know he was in town. It was always so lovely to see her excitement to see him. It made the long drive so worth it. Rick did not get there till late afternoon, so there were not many customers in the place. Which made Mary that much more enthusiastic when she rushed to the door and jumped upon him with a big hug and kiss. Mary's uncle looked from behind his window and waved a quick "Hey Rick."

Mary drew back from her hug position and held Rick's hand. "My mother is expecting you, so you can go give her a quick hello and go rest."

"And a shower," Rick said. "I am still a little rich from PT this morning and the five-hour, scorching drive."

"Oh, you are fine," Mary said as she did a fake sniff at him. "Oh. Maybe a shower is an excellent idea."

"Hey, don't rub it in."

"I would not even touch it, let alone rub it in, mister. Now get out of here, and I'll be home in a couple of hours."

One last kiss and Rick was on his way to say hi to Mary's mother.

Mary's mother was her usual friendly self and greeted Rick warmly with a big hug. She asked how the trip was and said how she was so happy to see him. Rick thought that Mary must not have shared too much about Atlanta, which was a good thing. Rick went up to his little garage hide-a-way, took a nice warm, sulfurous shower, and did a long-overdue nap.

Rick opened his eyes, and there were a pair of lovely brown eyes looking right at him. Mary's face was two inches away from his as she kneeled on the floor next to the bed.

After his mini shock wore off, he said in a low, sleepy voice, "You are never going to run out of creative ways to wake me up, are you?" Before Mary could say anything, Rick did a lunge at her lips and gave her a quick kiss.

"You looked so cute there sleeping that I didn't have the heart to wake you up right away. So, I just watched you for a few minutes."

"Now I am embarrassed," said Rick. "Hope I wasn't snoring."

"No, just looking cute."

Mary got up from the floor and sat on the bed next to Rick, while he stayed lying down.

Mary ran her hand through Rick's hair using her fingers as a comb. "You must have fallen asleep with wet hair, mister. You look like a regular, short-haired Albert Einstein.

"Very funny, now I am embarrassed a second time."

Mary still had her uniform on, and Rick was going to make a witty comment about it, but he thought that he had better leave that one alone, for now.

"So, what's up, my dear?"

"Well, you told my mother how you loved a good blackened red snapper, so guess what she is making you for supper tonight."

"Nice," said Rick, "and I bet she makes it wonderfully."

"She is also making you your hush puppies."

"Double nice," added Rick.

"You certainly have gotten on my mother's good side, young man, and I do love you for that."

"She was very nice to me when I arrived, so I assume you did not go into any details about Atlanta with her."

That got Rick a hit on the arm.

"No, I did not, and don't even joke about a thing like that."

"You are right. That would not be a good slip at the supper table, would it?"

Rick reached up and grabbed Mary and pulled her on top of him from her sitting position. They shared a nice, long, passionate kiss.

"I missed you, girl."

"I missed you too," Mary amplified "boy."

Mary rolled off Rick and jumped to the floor. She grabbed Rick's hand and dragged him up out of bed.

"Let's go, big boy, and mingle with the folks."

"Ok but let me get rid of this Einstein look first. Don't want to scare anybody."

They held hands all the way to the screen door but kept with tradition and let go when they entered the house.

The red snapper was terrific, and Rick could not stop eating or complimenting Joyce on it. Mary and her mother talked about cooking it while Carl had to know everything about the Atlanta band night. Rick told him how they did the same songs with a few modifications. And how great it was that he could practice beforehand. Carl, of course, knew the Kalamazoo song well and was impressed when Rick said they had pulled it off.

"What are you two kids doing tonight?" Carl asked Rick.

"I have no idea. I have to ask my social director," Rick said as he gave a quick head turn towards Mary.

"Well, I thought a movie might be nice if that is ok with you."

"Anything is fine," said Rick.

"Now wait a minute, son, you better find out what the movie is first. You know how these women can pick movies," Carl said.

"A, yes, you are right," Rick said with an authoritative tone and lowered his voice a few octaves. "It depends on what movie you want to see," then he amplified, "dear."

"Well, if you must know, I was thinking of *Harold and Maude.*"

"See, I told you, said Carl. You do know *Dirty Harry* is also playing."

Mary gave Carl an eye-roll, "Thanks for that, daddy."

"Anything is fine," another amplified, "dear," from Rick.

Rick and Mary started picking up dishes from the table and taking them to the kitchen.

"I will get these," said Joyce. "You two kids go out and have fun."

"Thanks for the lovely supper, Joyce," said Rick.

"You're welcome. Now get going!"

Outside Mary asked Rick, "Do you really want to see *Dirty Harry?*"

"No, anything really is fine. I was just trying to bond with your dad in there."

"I think you succeeded, again."

They went to *Harold and Maude.*

Mary got Rick up early, and they did their morning run along their usual route. After a quick breakfast and shower, they loaded their diving gear in the back of Mary's VW. Mary had insisted on driving this time as Rick had just driven five hours from Augusta. The old VW was a little cramped, but it all worked out, and Rick had to admit that he was a little tired of driving. Mary had still not told Rick about her surprise, only that SCUBA gear might be a little overkill. She also said that if they hit it right, it would be very cool. She also said that the closer to high noon, the better. Rick had no clue.

They left Lake City and headed south on Highway 47, past the Ichetucknee River area and Fort White. South of Fort White, Mary turned onto some nasty little roads that Rick's Jeep would have been better on. The vegetation was tall and thick, like most of the places Mary had taken Rick. They came into a clearing that looked like a make-shift parking area. One hundred feet away was an aqua colored body of water that flowed past the farthest trees. A small footpath followed the water into the trees. Mary pulled up to a downed tree and parked the car.

Mary got out of the car first, and Rick followed. They leaned their backs up against the car and looked at the water in front of them.

"Well, here we are."

"Ok," said Rick, "and just where is here?"

"This is the Gennie Spring area. Three main springs come out of here. That one over there is Little Devil, and downstream, almost to the Santa Fe River, there are two more. Devil's Eye and Devil's Ear. Our main goal is to get to Devil's Ear."

Mary noticed that Rick had a confused look on his face.

"Ok," Mary said as she grabbed a stick and did a drawing in the sand. "I am going to play teacher here. We are here. We will put on our diving gear here and float past Devil's Eye here, and then on to Devil's Ear, right here."

"Ok," said Rick, still sort of puzzled.

"You haven't been a student in a while, have you?"

"I don't know about that, teacher. You taught me a few things in Atlanta, as I recall."

That got Rick a nice hit on the arm.

"You are so bad."

"Actually, I think I was pretty good."

Rick got another hit, but this one was followed by a friendly kiss.

"Ok, class, let's pay attention here. Now it is going to be shallow all the way, some places only waist deep. It will be beautiful, and it will be nice to see it underwater like the Ichetucknee River. I have only snorkeled in here. My boyfriend in high school used to dive these caves a lot."

"Wait a minute," Rick interrupted, as he looked around the area, "I've been here before. Back when my college buddies and I were doing a little cave diving. We drove up here from Fort Myers and were going to explore one of these caves, but the place was loaded with police cars, ambulances, and fire trucks. We asked one of the officers, and he told us that three high school kids were lost in the caves. So, we had to leave."

"Wow," Mary said, "you do hear about that once in a while."

"We found out later that they went into the caves with no safety lines, and for lights, they wrapped regular flashlights in plastic bags. The water, of course, leaked into the lights, so they were in the dark and, with no safety lines, they had no way of knowing which way was out. One of them headed out the right way but ran out of air before he got out. The other two went farther into the cave until they ran out of air. It took them two days to find the one kid."

"And people ask me why I don't go diving in caves," said Mary. "Ok, class, let's get back to our lesson."

"Sorry, teach, it was just weird I didn't recognize this place earlier. That day and those kids stuck in my mind for a long time, especially when we did a cave dive shortly after that."

"I can see why," said Mary.

"Now our mission Rick, if you decide to accept it. I need to stop watching so much *Mission Impossible* with you, you know. We are heading out to Devil's Ear. Now don't miss it, or you'll end up in the Santa Fe River. We are going here because it is a spring that is maybe 20 feet wide but goes down deep into a series of caves. We are going down maybe 20 feet into the spring. As long as I can see the sky, I am ok down there. I recall there is an old log down there that we can sit on and look up at the surface."

"Can I ask why?" said Rick.

"Patience, young man, you are not a very good student, you know."

"Sorry, teach."

"As you can see, this water is crystal clear. Well, the Santa Fe is not. It is this yucky brown color from rotting vegetation and mangrove roots. What happens is the yucky brown water blends with this clear water where the two meet. The yucky water floats as a thin layer on the surface. It creates an amazing color display as the noon-time sun passes through it. I have tried looking at it many times, but only with snorkeling equipment and holding breath. Holding breath while trying to look up did not work well. So, I'm excited to just sit down there and see if we can get a show. What do you think, Ricky boy?"

"Whew, I think I got all of that, and it sounds pretty amazing."

"Well, let's do it then. The sun is high," said Mary.

They dragged out their tanks and gear and started strapping in.

"We will have to swim back against the current if that is ok," said Mary. "We can walk back but carrying tanks wouldn't be fun."

"No problem," Rick said. "It should be an easy swim with tanks on, plus we can get some more underwater time in."

"You are my kind of guy," said Mary.

They walked into the water on the white sandy bottom till they were waist deep. Before they put their masks down and mouthpieces in, they shared a friendly kiss.

"I love you, mister," said Mary.

"I love you too, ma'am."

In a stream of bubbles and stirred up sand, they started downstream. Very little kicking was needed as the current carried them along at a slow pace. As usual, they held each other's hand as they floated. They passed the Little Devil spring, which was just a tiny hole coming out of the sandy bottom There was a lot of vegetation around it, but the spring itself was mostly sand and limestone rocks. Both sides of the river had a lot of greenery, where the fish were hanging out. A six-inch painted turtle crossed their path right in front of them. It was not long before they came to The Devil's Eye spring. A larger round hole coming out of the bottom, like Little Devil spring but much larger. They swam over the top of it, and they both went down and hung out at the entrance for a few minutes. They could see down about twenty feet but then it was just darkness after that.

Just a short distance more, and they were at the Devil's Ear. Mary was right. It was only waist deep, so they surfaced and stood on the bottom. It was a rocky bottom, not sandy. They both pulled their masks up onto their heads and took out their mouthpieces.

"Well, what do you think?" asked Mary.

"That was not very far at all. I was expecting a long swim."

"I told you SCUBA gear would be an overkill, but I hope the cave will be worth it."

They were standing right next to the spring and the strong current was obviously beating on them. The trees and vegetation were very close as the water area was not that big. The water was not much larger than the spring itself.

"Ok. Are you ready, Sweetie?" Mary said as she pulled down her mask.

They swam over to the spring and floated over the top of it for a few minutes. They just looked down into the big hole. It was at least twenty feet in diameter, so there was plenty of room for the two of them to descend side-by-side. Mary was right. At the bottom, maybe 25 feet down, was a log that went all the way across the shaft. It was one big log. Another 20 feet down was a small bottom that was all white sand. The white sand reflected the surface light nicely, so the whole spring was very bright. Mary did a surface dive straight down into the shaft. Rick followed in her bubbles. Mary stopped her descent so she could clear her ears, Rick did the same. Mary continued down until she got to the log, where she stopped and looked up at Rick. She motioned to him to stop and pointed at the log just before she sat on it.

They sat on the log and leaned against the rock sides of the shaft. Mary motioned to Rick to look up. They both looked up at the ear-shaped opening above them, holding hands, of course. All that could be seen was the bright opening. The surrounding rocks were all dark, almost like looking through a telescope. The water was so clear, and the sun was so high that you could see the tree trunks and the leaves on the trees surrounding the spring. They looked like they were growing out the sides of the opening. The turquoise water made the rocks at the top of the shaft glow a blue green. The center of the opening was completely clear except for a green tint from the tree vegetation. After about ten minutes, the clear green center turned a bright yellow, but the turquoise outside stayed. Then it turned back to the green. Five minutes later, the center turned yellow, but the far-right had tinges of red and orange. You could still see the trees through all the colors. Then it cleared again. It stayed clear for at least another five minutes. Then a burst of yellows came in, followed by orange, and then a giant cloud of red. The shaft got dark and very eerie. Mary squeezed Rick's hand very tight. The outer left edges were still the bright turquoise, but the rest looked more like a cloud at sunset in the sky rather than a liquid cloud in the water. It was amazing. Then within five minutes, it cleared again.

Mary squeezed Rick's hand, and when he looked over at her, she gave a finger up. Rick figured she had had enough after that last dark color display when the light went out. He did not blame her.

They headed for the surface.

They swam out of the hole and off to the sides, where they both stood up in waist-deep water. They took their mouthpieces out and lifted their masks on top of their heads.

"Now that was pretty darn cool," Rick said. "You were right. Sitting there and watching the whole show was much better than trying to dive up and down, snorkeling."

"I did figure that," Mary Said. "I don't know why I or any of my friends had never done that before."

"Thanks so much for sharing that with me. I loved it," Rick said as he stepped over and gave Mary a kiss.

He caught his swim fin on Mary's and almost sent them both tumbling into the water.

"Ok," Rick said as he caught Mary before she fell over. "How about we head back upstream?"

"Sounds good," Mary had her mask on already and was starting to submerge.

They were back at the old VW and taking off their diving gear in a very short time. They set everything in the sun to dry out, and Mary brought out a blanket and spread it out in the sand next to the car's passenger-side door. She then set out a lunch of cheese, crackers, and some fresh sliced mango and oranges wedges on the blanket.

"This is pretty nice there, girl."

"Why, thank you, sir, and for a perfect pairing, we have this fine two-month-old Boones Farm Strawberry wine."

Mary poured it into two paper Dixie cups and handed one to Rick.

"Here's to another great adventure," Mary said.

"Thank you so much. It was a good one," Rick said as he leaned over and gave Mary a kiss.

They ate lunch, drank wine, and talked about the spring and the color show for a long time. After lunch, Rick and Mary dropped down together on the blanket and let the sun warm their bodies. The sun was very hot, but their bodies were still chilled and wrinkled from the spring water. Mary rolled over on top of Rick, and they shared a warm and passionate series of kisses. Mary was in her two-piece bikini and Rick in his trunks, so they both became extremely excited when Mary said, "Have you ever done it in a VW, mister?"

"A, no," came a shocked stutter from Rick.

Mary jumped up and grabbed Rick by the hand and pulled him up off the blanket. Still holding his hand, she flipped the tilt-down seat lever with her other hand, and the seat folded down into the back seat. Mary then spread her body down on the seat and physically pulled Rick on top of her. The feeling of warm, sunbaked flesh against each other pushed them over the limit of excitement. Just as Rick and Mary started maneuvering each other's swimsuits, the roar of four screaming cars full of high school kids pulled up next to them. A quick scramble off the seat and back on the blanket took place in a millisecond, and they were back drinking Boones Farm. Flushed, out of breath, frustrated, and laughing hysterically.

"I think that might be a sign that we should get going, don't you think, dear," said Mary.

"Yeah, I bet your mother sent them."

That got Rick a nice hit on the arm.

They packed up their gear and headed back to Lake City.

Rick brought up how Ted wanted to come down the following weekend and do a cave dive on the ride back.

"Would that be, ok?" Rick asked.

"Of course, that would be great."

"I also mentioned your friend Sandy to Ted. I told him that she loved to camp, fish, and hunt. Oh, and that she had an old four-wheel-drive Ford Bronco. After I told him all that, he really was excited to meet her. Hell, I am excited to meet her."

Mary took one hand off the wheel and gave Rick a good hit on his arm.

"Ouch, that was a good one. I'm just kidding, you know, I love you, my sweet," Rick said with a hint of sarcasm.

"You better, my sweet," Mary answered back with the same sarcastic voice.

"Maybe she would like to go with us on the dive. We could make a day out of it," Rick said.

"That sounds great also. I will give Sandy a call tomorrow. We talked about her meeting Ted a while back, and she seemed excited about the whole thing. Especially after I told her what a wonderful soldier boy I had."

"And who would that be?" asked Rick.

"Nobody you would know."

"Well, you need to introduce me sometime."

"Oh, I will. I will also call Dave tomorrow."

"Dave?" Rick asked.

"You know, Dave, my old high school boyfriend. The cave diver."

"Oh, I forgot you did mention him."

"We are still good friends. He married another good friend of mine from high school. They have a two-year-old and another one on the way. He doesn't cave dive anymore, but he could remind me where a good place to go would be."

"That would be great," said Rick. "Could you also ask if he has any old safety lines and lights we could use? Those are the only things that I don't have. My other cave diving buddies always had that stuff."

"No problem, I know he would be happy to loan you any equipment you needed. He is a very nice guy, and he sure did love his cave diving."

Rick and Mary got back to Lake City late afternoon, which gave each of the time to shower and clean up before supper. Rick snuck in a short power nap, something he learned in the Army. You always caught a nap anytime there was some free time because you never knew when the next sleep was coming.

Mary woke Rick up by silently crawling in bed with him. Rick woke from his sleep with the feeling of Mary's lips on his neck and the smell of her freshly shampooed hair on his cheek. She put her arm over his chest, and her leg wrapped over his legs and drove herself into Rick's hip.

"Get up, sleepyhead. Supper is almost on the table."

"Not before your sleeping beauty gets a wake-up kiss."

Mary rolled over on top of Rick, gave him a long and passionate kiss, and then rolled off him quickly and jumped to the floor.

"Come on, sweetie, we need to go," Mary said as she grabbed Rick's arm and pulled him up so he could sit up on the side of the bed.

"Ok, drill sergeant. Let me run a comb through this hair first and slap some water in my face."

"Ok, soldier, but double-time it."

It was another delightful meal with Mary's parents. Joyce made an excellent cornmeal breaded catfish with homemade coleslaw and baked beans. Rick asked Mary's parents if it would be ok if Ted slept on the garage couch next weekend. They, of course, said yes. Rick was once again reminded how meals with family could be delightful and fun. Not to mention the family bonding time that seemed so precious and was so lacking in his family. Another reason that Mary was so good for him.

After supper, Rick and Mary helped clean up the kitchen. They went to Rick's little hide-a-way above the garage and watched TV. *Mary Tyler Moore*, of course for Mary, followed by *Bob Newhart*. That was enough, and they turned off the television and just sat on the couch, in the dark, cuddled in each other's arms, watching the moon rising halfway up the sky. There was a nice warm breeze coming through the screens. A warm breeze that only Florida can have at night.

"This is pretty nice," Rick said as he pulled Mary closer.

"It doesn't get much better," Mary answered as she pressed her head harder onto Rick's chest.

After a long silence, Mary softly said, "I think we need to talk about the next few weeks, don't you?"

"I know," said Rick. "I think it has been something in the back of our minds, probably since we fell in love."

"Yes, it has."

Rick thought a moment, then said, "I think our love affair has been going forward so fast that we have had no time to stop and think about the consequences of it all and where we were heading."

"I believe we were having too much fun and laughing way too hard to face the reality of it all," said Mary.

"That could have been largely my fault. Throughout high school, college, and the Army, I have conditioned myself not to think too far ahead. The future has always been so uncertain. My hometown was a poor, blue collar place where not many of us went to college. After high school, my friends and I, always figured we would get drafted and possibly end up face down in a rice patty somewhere. That is why none of us had great grades and we partied way too much. This eventual fate that was locked into our subconscious, instilled in us the one-day-at-a-time attitude."

Mary didn't say anything. She just squeezed Rick's hand tighter.

"You have to keep going forward with your dream of finishing school and getting your degree in Chicago."

"I know."

"And for me, for the first time since Junior High school, I do not have the draft, the Army, or Vietnam hanging over my head."

"I know."

"And I need to keep going forward with that."

"I know," Mary said again.

"We knew upfront that we would be going forward in our relationship but that it would reach a point that there would be no more forward, just stopping. If there is no going forward in a relationship, there is no relationship left."

"I know that too, but we made the mistake of falling in love."

"That was no mistake. It's been the most wonderful thing in my life," Rick added.

"I know, mine too," said Mary. "I just don't want us to end, and it's going to get more complicated over the next few weeks."

They did a long, hard kiss.

"I do love you so much," said Mary, as she started to cry.

The first time Rick had seen Mary even come close to crying. He did not like to see her this way. He was tearing up also.

"I love you too," said Rick. "That is the most wonderful part of all this, and it is ending up being the worse part. I would not change one single thing with this love affair of ours, however."

"I know, dear, it has certainly been a whirlwind affair, hasn't it?"

"The adventures, love, and laughs we crammed into a short time, most people don't experience what we have in a lifetime," Rick said.

"I know. My parents sure have gotten used to you and love you to death, especially my dad. I think he likes you like the son he never had."

"They are certainly nice people, although I thought I was dead when I first met them."

"So did I," said Mary as she was crying a little less now. Rick reached into his back pocket and gave her his handkerchief.

"Ok," Mary continued. "In three weeks, we will be going our separate ways, but let's keep doing what we have been doing till then. Let's keep loving each other and laughing and playing and just enjoying each other like we do so well. Deal?"

"Deal," said Rick as he pulled Mary close again, and they kissed very hard for a very long time. Which brought Mary's tears back.

Rick rustled up his best Bogart, "We'll always have Atlanta, sweetheart."

"Yes, we will," answered Mary, giving Rick another kiss.

"Here's looking at you, kid," Rick added.

"That was pretty a good, Bogie."

"Pretty good, that was damn good."

They sat there for another thirty minutes enjoying each other's warmth before Mary went back to the house. They were now feeling both better and worse.

The following day, Rick was awoken by a quick knock on his door.

"Hey, anybody up in there?"

Before Rick could answer, the door flew open, and Mary ran over to Rick's bed. Sleeping on the sheets made it easy for Mary to jump on the bed and snuggled next to him. In just her nightshirt with nothing underneath, she put her leg over the top of his. Rick turned his whole body towards her.

"What are you doing here, young lady," Rick said.

"Just coming in to say good morning to you, my sweet."

"I think it is a little more than "good morning" dressed like that, my sweet. I don't think your parents would care for this type of behavior." Rick said with a twist of humor.

"I don't think they would either, but they are at church and going out to breakfast for the next couple of hours."

Rick was hard as soon as Mary nestled next to him, but he knew exactly what was on Mary's mind with her last statement. His hardness now broke through the opening on his boxer shorts.

"My, my," said Mary. "Someone is happy to see me again."

Mary went down and pulled off Rick's boxers and pulled her nightshirt over her head. She then took her naked body down on Rick and excited him more with her warm mouth. Just when Rick thought he had had enough, Mary stopped and moved her body up to him far enough to give him a passionate kiss. Still, side by side, facing each other, Mary threw her leg high over Rick's hip so that his hardness could enter her. It fit well, and they started their motion of love. The passion and the wild movement continued for a seemly very long time. Still facing each other on their sides, they both came to a very happy ending. Staring into each other's eyes, out of breath and out of energy, they kissed a kiss that was probably their most passionate and loving one yet. They embraced there for a very long time. They both were thinking how wonderful it was being so close to each other. Still, also they were thinking of their talk the night before and their uncertain future together.

"Ok, big boy," said Mary, "and I meant that as a compliment," as she reached down and grabbed hold of Rick.

Rick jumped when she did. "Hey," is all he said.

"I think I would like to hit the road before your parents get back. I don't think I can hide this glow from them."

"And what am I supposed to do with mine, mister."

"You can blame it on the heat, I guess."

"Ok, why don't you get yourself together and pack your stuff in your Jeep. Come in the house before you leave, and I will make you a nice breakfast."

"Sounds great," said Rick, as he watched Mary put back on her skimpy nightshirt. He got excited again.

"I will try and call Sandy and Dave so we can find out about next weekend before you take off."

"Ok."

Rick watched Mary exit the door. "Damn, I do love that girl," he mumbled in a low voice to himself.

Mary made Rick a wonderful breakfast of biscuits and gravy with some strong coffee. She also packed coffee and a snack for the road. She got ahold of both Sandy and Dave. Sandy was up for meeting Ted and making the dive trip. Dave was excited to hear from Mary and was happy to loan out some of his gear. Divers are like that, except for loaning out regulators.

Rick and Mary did a very long goodbye, and Rick was again off for the long haul to Augusta. This drive was going to be a long and deep thinking one.

CHAPTER 13
Ted and Sandy

It was a relatively easy week for Rick playing Army as it was his last week teaching, so most of it was spent testing. He still had his morning PT sessions, but he found those relaxing. He met with Ted one night at the Officer's Club, where they had supper and talked about the weekend. Afterward, they organized their dive gear so it would be ready to go on Friday morning.

Rick was hit with some reality training when he was ordered to report the Transition Assistance Office, where he picked up his out-processing papers. It was a huge folder, not much smaller than the Bible. That was filled with a multitude of documents that all had to be signed. Seems it was harder to get out of the Army than it was to get in. Of course, it was easy getting in as all you needed was a draft notice. There was a form for every check-out point. Points like another physical, dentist, supply (to turn in all gear), transition counseling sessions, payroll, and many more. The final and best form was DA Form 31. This was the final request for leave form. It finally hit Rick that he was actually going to be out of the Army, and it was an excellent feeling.

By the time Rick and Ted got the Jeep loaded on Friday and checked off post, it was 1000-hours. They did not get into Lake City until well after 1500-hours. They stopped by the Diner, and Rick and Mary shared their usual exciting greeting. Rick re-introduced Ted to Mary. They went on to Rick's little garage house, where they both took a needed shower. Ted did not care for the sulfur water. They both settled in for a quick and easy nap.

Rick heard Mary drive up, so he quickly hopped out of bed and ran down to meet her. He did not want to disturb Ted but mainly wanted to have his usual hello with Mary. A greeting that was looked forward to all week. He was once again not disappointed. They did a long hard kiss at the bottom of his stairs.

"How are you doing, soldier boy?"

"Doing just fine now, ma'am."

"I missed you," Mary said as she still had her arms around Rick's neck, and their lips were inches apart.

"I missed you also."

They did another long kiss.

"Ok, enough of that mussy stuff," Mary said as she pushed herself away off Rick's chest. "We have to get going."

"What are we doing?"

"I told Sandy that we would meet her at Lum's at seven o'clock. Have you ever been to a Lum's?"

"Come on, I lived at that place when I was in college down in Fort Meyers. Cheap, good food, and of course, great beers in those ice-cold frosty mugs."

"You go get Ted, and I will go change."

"Change? You mean you are not going to wear that sexy pink uniform?"

"As sexy as it is, I don't think so, smarty. I don't want Lum's to think I am on the payroll."

"Now move it, troop," Mary said as she tip-toed up and gave Rick a quick kiss."

"Yes, drill sergeant."

All three of them piled into Mary's VW, and they were off to Lum's.

They got a booth where Rick and Mary sat together facing the door so Mary could see when Sandy arrived. Sandy walked through the door a short time later. Mary, of course, jumped up to greet her with a big hug.

Rick could get a nice view of her as she walked towards the table while Ted would have to be surprised at the last moment.

She was a tall woman, maybe 5'8" with a definite outdoor look. She was slender and had a red, white, black plaid cotton top and a short denim skirt. Cowboy boots down below and a Stetson hat on top. She had blondish red hair. When she got closer, Rick could see her blue eyes and her natural look. Like Mary, she also needed very little makeup to look beautiful. By the look on Ted's face when he stood up to meet her, Rick knew that Ted would be revisiting Lake City.

After introductions, Sandy sat down next to Ted. The waitress quickly came by, and they ordered four frosty schooners of beer. Lum's was famous for its international beers, so everyone got something different. Rick loved his stout.

Mary broke the conversation ice, "How are your two horses doing, Sandy?"

"Wonderfully," said Sandy. "My mare is due in about four months."

"Ted is from Montana, you know," said Rick.

"Really, do you have a ranch there?" asked Sandy with a bit of excitement in her voice.

"A, no," said Ted, "my parents actually live in the town of Bozeman. My aunt does have a ranch up in Great Falls, where I spent much of my summers working. And riding, by the way."

The beers came, and they made a toast.

"Here's to a great adventure day tomorrow," said Rick.

Clink, clink, clink, clink.

They ordered a round of Lum's famous hot dogs boiled in beer, and Rick and Ted also ordered a Lumburger, a BBQ burger served on an egg bun. And, of course, the onion rings and fries.

"So, Rick," Sandy said, "I hear you are about out of the Army."

"Yes, ma'am."

"Any plans?"

Rick knew how women talk and that she and Mary had been talking about him, so he had to be very careful.

"Not really. One day at a time." He squeezed Mary's hand a little tighter under the table.

"Well, our girl here is going to the big city of Chicago."

"So I have heard," said Rick.

"Ted, I hear you are getting out soon also," said Mary to change the subject.

"Six months," said Ted.

"What are you going to be doing?" asked Sandy.

"One day at a time, also. The same thing Rick and I have been doing for the past few years."

Trying to change the subject again, Mary said, "So about tomorrow. I got directions and equipment from Dave last week. I thought we could leave early to avoid the heat as there will be a little hike involved. Does that sound ok?"

Everyone agreed.

"Sandy has a Scout, so if it is ok, Ted can ride with her, and Rick and I can take his Jeep."

"Sounds like a good plan," said Sandy. "Mary and I have packed a lunch and lots of beer."

"Now that sounds like an excellent plan," said Ted.

"All settled then," said Rick.

Clink, clink, clink, clink.

After another round of beers, Sandy and Ted loosened up and the joking around and laughter flowed.

Ted paid the check, and Rick picked up the tip.

Ted was paying the check when Sandy said, "Hey Ted, how about you and I go out and do a little dancing and let these two have some alone time?"

"I would love to," said Ted.

Out of the corner of his eye, Rick saw Mary mouthing to Sandy a subtle, thank you.

Mary had Rick drive the VW back home, and they went up to the garage apartment. Rick grabbed a couple more beers, and they sat together on the couch.

After a long kiss, Rick said, "How are you doing?"

"I am doing ok. I told Uncle Bob I would be quitting in two weeks. He knew I would be but was surprised that it was so soon. He has been such a great uncle to me over the years. Especially with the job he gave me. He pays me much more than I should be getting."

"That's pretty cool," said Rick. "Reality hit me also this week as I got my processing-out papers. I start signing out next week."

A long silence.

"I am starting to feel a little trapped and sad as the end of our relationship is closing in on us," said Mary sadly.

"I have been feeling the same way," Rick added. "Claustrophobic might even be a better word, not with our love affair, but because there does not seem to be a way out for us,"

"It is pretty strange how we are each making a major life change at the same time, isn't it?" Mary said.

"I know. And how we met each other right at the moment that it was all happening."

"And fell in love," whispered Mary.

"I know, not very good timing on our part, was it?"

"No, it wasn't," said Mary.

"Maybe it would have been better if I had not stopped for that coffee at your Diner."

"Don't you say that mister," Mary said with a loud harshness in her voice. "The time we have spent together has been the happiest in my life, and I would not have traded it for anything."

Mary eyes were now filling.

Rick turned her towards him and touched her cheek. "They have been the happiest for me also. Even if our love affair is not going forward, we will always have what we had, and that can never be taken from us. I do love you; you know."

"Yes, I know, and I love you. It is just that our timing sucks so bad."

They did a long, passionate kiss.

Rick's eyes joined Mary's. They both lowered their eyelids to hide the tears from each other. Sitting in the darkness, with hands locked and arms wrapped, they continued to love each other.

CHAPTER 14
The Cave Dive

Even though the morning sun was just starting to flicker through the tall mangrove trees in the eastern sky, everyone could tell that it was going to be one of those hot and muggy days. Of course, you would not expect anything different when playing in the swamps of central Florida in mid-summer. Rick had just driven his Jeep, and Sandy her Bronco, as far as they could down a rutted path that was a stretch, to be called a road. The dense swamp, at this point, could not support a road, so the rest of the trip would be on foot. Once parking spots were found, everyone sat in the vehicles and stared at a massive wall of vegetation in front of them. There seem there might be foot paths in the wall of green, but the vegetation in this area grew so fast that they were almost invisible.

Mary was the first out of the jeep and, with a bit of little girl enthusiasm, was already running to find a trail.

After running back and forth along the green wall looking for potential openings, she finally stopped at one.

"This is the one we want," Mary yelled back at everyone with an authoritative tone.

Everyone began loading their bodies up with supplies and gear and started to hike down the not-so-obvious path, that Mary had found. Mary and Sandy led the way toting the cooler. After traveling a good twenty minutes with only heavy breathing as the conversation, Mary broke the silence.

"We have at least a quarter of a mile to go yet before we reach the pond," Mary said, with an out-of-breath voice.

"Thank you for sharing that with us," Rick answered back. "Couldn't you have just said that it was just around that next scrub oak bush? You know, keep the carrot right in front of us instead of way down the road."

"The pond is right around that next scrub oak bush, everyone," Mary answered back instantly with a sarcastic tone.

Ted had missed the beginnings of the conversation, so he said, "Great, I am tired of this forced march."

Everyone laughed when Sandy told Ted that Mary was just kidding.

It was a typical Florida Path. The vegetation was so abundant and grew so fast that something green, rubbed or poked, with every step. There was also the constant scurrying and slithering of creatures along the sides of the trail, trying to escape the new intruders. Most people from the city would be alarmed at such things but everyone in the group were well seasoned swamp travelers.

Walking through the thick undergrowth was terrible enough but carrying heavy diving equipment and camping supplies made it that much more difficult. This type of adventure was not new to anyone, so the complaining was kept at a minimum. Any whining was qualified with high amounts of humor and ridicule.

Mary was directly ahead of Rick. He was still always impressed by how well she knew every back road and trail in these swamps. Rick could not help thinking how lovely she looked in her two-piece bathing suit. Of course, he could only see her below the waist as the upper half of her body was covered with a backpack and safety ropes. Her long brown hair could still be seen peeking through all the gear. Rick's mind wandered briefly, thinking how her beautiful hair could only be fully appreciated when it flowed over him and swallowed most of her pillow. She was walking alongside Sandy with the cooler between them. It was evident that it was heavily weighted with supplies as the muscles in both their forearms were being stretched to their limits and their bodies tilted at an extreme angle away from the cooler. The stress of the load was, however, amplifying each of their feminine motions, which made for a delightful sight.

"You are not watching the trail, are you dear," Mary yelled back at Rick without turning her head.

"Oh, of course, I am, my sweet," Rick answer back, "what else could I possibly be looking at?"

"Our asses, you dirty old man," Mary answered back with a humorous tone and a forced extreme back and forth motion of her posterior side.

Everyone laughed as best they could under the physical strain.

Ted and Rick were loaded down with diving equipment, so they had their own struggles to deal with. It was always amazing how heavy diving gear was out of the water. The tanks and weight belts were heavy, and the bulkiness of the masks, fins, and wet suits made things awkward to carry. The soft sand and heavy undergrowth made it that much more difficult. They constantly had to turn sideways or step over large roots to stay on the path.

The thick vegetation was gradually opening into a small sandy beach area next to a swampy body of water. They had finally arrived. The whole pond was less than five hundred feet in diameter and circling around the outer edges were masses of floating vegetation. It was all a bright green, except for a small area at the center. This patch at the center was radiating a bright aqua color. That was the spring that housed the cave entrance. The entire pond looked like a giant green eyeball with an aqua pupil. The only areas with no vegetation were the beach they were standing on and a small sandy beach at the far side of the pond. The rest of the area, surrounding the water was composed of various low-lying plants and bushes. These were mixed in with a scattering of sixty-foot-tall trees. These all joined together to frame the rest of the area around the pond. It was obvious that the way they came in was the only way to enter the area or get to the water. Two tall mangrove trees were growing out of the water on the shores closest to the cave opening. A downed, floating mangrove trunk , spanned almost the whole northern side of the pond. It was indeed a rustic and beautiful spot. The contrast of all the green and the bright aqua cave entrance was striking.

Everyone dropped their equipment and settled down with their backs on top of the warm sand. They stayed motionless for a well-deserved rest. After less than a minute of breath catching, Mary crawled over and hopped on top of Rick's upturned body. She grabbed both of his wrists and pinned him to the sand like they were in a wrestling match. All her weight was now on Rick's stomach. She leaned over and brought her head down to within an inch of his.

"I have always heard that you knew how to show a girl a good time, she said, and this proves it." She lifted one hand off Rick's wrist and pointed to the marks left by the backpack straps on her arm.

She grabbed Rick's wrist again, lowered herself down, and gave him a long kiss.

"Just kidding," she said.

"Just kidding, yes, but it was certainly enough to get Rick his usual excitement whenever Mary got close to him.

They all lodged on the warm sand for a long while, talking and laughing.

Rick broke up the socializing, "We need to get in that water, Ted, while the sun is high, and the visibility is good."

"I know," said Ted with a reluctant tone. "It is so nice just lying in this soft sand."

Being next to that nice looking lady over there would have nothing to do with that, would it?" Rick said.

Ted was speechless, Sandy smiled, and Rick got a jab in the ribs.

"You are so bad," Mary said. "They do make a sweet looking couple, don't they?"

Mary helped Rick with his diving equipment like they had gotten used to doing for each other. Even though she was not diving today, she seemed to enjoy the adventures as much as he did. The wet suit was always the hardest. Both Rick and Ted were wearing a thin top suit, as they knew they would be down in the cooler spring water, and the jagged rocks would be rough on bare skin. Rick and Ted did a quick check of their equipment. Rick had experienced a few close calls with faulty diving gear, so he was always overly safety conscious. Dave's underwater lights were of good quality, and Mary had installed new batteries. Along with the lights, Rick also had both of them carrying underwater flares as backup lights. Most cave diving groups attach one safety line per group, but Rick insisted on having one for each. It would make things more awkward and complicated in tight areas, but the thought of being in an underwater cave in the dark, with no safety line to the surface, was always a horrible thought. Rick also learned from his cave diving friends that you always have someone onshore guarding the lines in case some passer-by thinks it would be funny to toss them into the cave. This was Mary and Sandy's job, although there were probably no one around for miles.

Once suited up, Mary gave Rick a long kiss, and Sandy felt obligated to do the same with Ted. Ted did not mind. Rick and Ted start to walk backward into the water of the pond. It was not water but felt and looked more like a green Jell-O that was just setting up. Green slime and algae started percolating up around their legs. Small green leaves about the size of baby green peas covered the entire surface of the water. Their own weight, plus the weight of their heavy diving equipment, caused them to sink down into the bottom sediments up to their calves. They squished into layers of decomposed plant life and mud. With each step, pockets of hydrogen sulfide swamp gas were released from the bottom. These gas bubbles rose to the surface around their legs, expelling a pungent odor.

"This smells worse than your dirty army socks," Rick turned and yelled back at Ted.

"Not any worse than your beer farts," Ted retaliated with a nervous laugh.

Like he was ignoring the comment, Rick shouted back at Ted so he could hear above their sloshing. "I bet this shit has been waiting for us down there for the last hundred years."

"Maybe more than that," answered Ted.

It was slow and demanding work wading backwards through the Jell-O. Their path was clearly marked by the parting of the green blanket of vegetation. Flowing into this path was black water and mud rising from the bottom.

"I feel like Moses parting the Red Sea," said Rick.

"I bet he did not have swamp gas to deal with, answered Ted.

Like undone shoelaces, the red safety lines wove their way through the green, muddy water. The open water where the spring water percolated to the surface was their destination, but it was still thirty feet away. It was much closer to the other side of the pond but the thick underbrush and trees there would have made it impossible to enter from that side. Walking through the slime was the only way in. Black water and green slime were now all the way up to their chests. It was now getting too deep to walk.

"How about we get out of this shit and start playing fish," Rick said to Ted as his chin sank below the surface.

"An excellent idea," Ted replied with his mask already pulled down over his face.

Rick could not really see the shore over the green vegetation, but he gave Mary a quick wave before he pulled down his mask and bit his mouthpiece. He didn't know if she saw him or not.

They each did an air-check and then submerged through the green Jell-O into the black water.

Once under the surface, they were surprised by crystal clear water. The visibility had to be at least a hundred feet. There was a beautiful green tinge on everything, as the sun passed through the emerald vegetation on the surface. It was indeed an incredible sight. Rick tapped Ted's shoulder and pointed towards a water moccasin that was lazily weaving in and out of the floating plants on the surface. It was at least thirty feet away, but Ted's eyes still got large with fear. Rick had many stories of being in the water with snakes but found that most of the time they leave you alone. Vietnam had cured him of worrying about snakes as they were everywhere you stepped. He did still hate when they scared the crap out of you.

On the other hand, Ted was obviously not a big snake fan. He aggressively pointed down to the cave, indicating that he was ready to get off the surface. The cave opening was illuminated by a bright blue beam from a hole in the vegetation on the surface. The cave's mouth was at least thirty feet wide, so they both easily fit through the opening. The currents were powerful coming out of the spring, so they struggled swimming into the main cavern. Maybe swimming was not the correct word as underwater mountain climbing had a better fit. Even with weight belts on, they had to grab rock after rock chunks to pull themselves down into the cave. The surface pond's calmness certainly did not indicate how strong the springs current was. With the current, rock handling, and swim fins, the visibility became almost zero from all the stirred-up particles. Getting out their lights made it more difficult, as their underwater mountain climbing was now one-handed. After about thirty feet of upside-down scrambling, the tunnel opened into a large cavern, where the current seemed to almost stop. Once into the cavern and past the stirred-up silt, the visibility became seemingly infinite again. Their light beams could now see all the cavern walls and the many tunnels branching off. The bottom of the cavern was covered entirely with a layer of white sand. The sand almost looked like a big fluffy cloud that reflected the light from their lanterns in all directions. The reflection gave everything a bright blue color. There were at least half dozen tunnels leading off into the depths from the main cavern. Rick tapped Ted on the shoulder, pointed to all of them, and shrugged his shoulders, indicating which one they should take. Ted replied by putting both hands up in the air. Ted then shone his light across each tunnel before pointing at one of the larger ones and motioning to Rick that that was the one. With a sweeping motion of his hand, followed by a slight bow towards Rick and the tunnel, he indicated that Rick should go first.

The opening was over ten feet wide, so there was plenty of room for them to enter without hitting the sides or bottom, avoiding stirring up loose silt. The rich blue color of the main cavern had given way to a dull brownish green. The current was minimal in this tunnel, giving a calming, peaceful feeling as there was no struggling to move forward. The tunnel was now almost horizontal. Which was nice, as their air bubbles were not floating around their faces, as it had been during the descent. The sides and ceiling were jagged with almost the appearance of lava rock, not limestone. The tunnel floor had a narrow stream of sand flowing on it. It appeared like a river winding in and out of the jagged rocks. Rick turned and gave a thumbs-up towards Ted, and he gave an enthusiastic thumbs-up back. As they headed deeper into the cave, most of their fears and anxieties had subsided, with the calming effect of the apparent silence.

The cave was starting to narrow, but there was still plenty of room around them to comfortably swim without touching the sides or ceiling. There seemed to be no side tunnels off this main cavern, which explained the reasonably calm current. Now that Rick was comfortable with the surroundings in the cave, he started appreciating the wonder and amazement of it all. *There are so few people that ever get to see something like this.* Rick thought. *Maybe we are even the first people to ever see these rocks, this sand, and this whole cave. We are a modern-day Ponce de Leon, looking for the fountain of youth.* Rick started thinking about Mary, lying up in the sun, holding onto his safety line. He wondered if she was thinking about him and how she was holding his life in her hands. *I am her puppet, and she is controlling the strings. Do I want that?*

Rick's hypnotic thoughts were interrupted quickly by the muffled sound of his tank valve scraping the ceiling of the cave. The tunnel had narrowed very quickly, so narrow that there were only a few inches of clearance all around him. He stopped so he could turn around to see whether Ted had also noticed the narrowing. He could not turn his head around enough to look back, and in the process of trying, a large amount of silt was churned up. Since there was no current to flush it out, the sediment just hung around his face mask. Visibility was instantly degraded from crystal clear to almost zero. Rick and Ted's light beams illuminated every tiny silt particle like thousands of little lanterns, amplifying the anxiety of not seeing.

Rick decided to move forward to get them out of the silt cloud. Once in clear water, Rick tried again to look back at Ted for some suggestions but could not turn around to see him. The tunnel had now gotten narrower yet, so Rick could barely move, let alone look back. Rick thought *I guess the decision is up to me. Do we keep going forward and hope that the tunnel will widen enough to turn around, or do we try and back out?* Rick knew that they could not back out without taking off their tanks and dragging them behind them. That was not a pleasant thought. The tunnel was so narrow that he doubted they could even get their tanks off. There still was a current coming up the tunnel and that told Rick that something had to be ahead. So, Rick thought the best thing to do was to keep going forward.

He could not signal Ted, so he was hoping he would just follow him. Rick could only imagine what Ted was thinking. His visibility had to be almost zero, with Rick stirring up everything ahead of him. Ted also did not have the luxury of seeing ahead as to where they were going. Maybe that was a blessing at that point. The passage was not opening as they swam deeper. In fact, it was getting smaller. Rick's stomach was hugging the sandy floor as he slowly moved, and his tank was still hitting the ceiling. The beam of light coming from his lantern was narrow, but the cavern was so small and narrow that it lit up all four walls ahead of him. A good indication that the cavern was indeed getting narrower yet. The center of the tunnel was still only black. Rick started consciously fighting off claustrophobic ideas, for that would be disastrous at this point. He had been in many frightening situations before, so he had a system of mental exercises that he practiced. He always tried to think of something else, something pleasant. Amazingly, at that moment, he thought about Mary and how he maybe was feeling claustrophobic in their relationship. Not being able to move forward with things. *Thank you, Mary, for that thought, as it certainly does not help me much,* Rick thought. Then he just thought about Mary's face, her laugh, and that smile. The vision snapped him out of panic mode. It was a brief relief as his mind now started thinking of equipment problems. Malfunction of equipment that he seemed to have had more often in the past than he cared to. *What if one of our regulator's malfunctions?* He thought. *There is no way that we could turn to each other and buddy breath. There is not even enough room to remove our tanks if we needed to.* Rick quickly tried to return to happy thoughts again. *Mary in the warm sand on the surface, her long hair, her brown eyes, tanned body, she loves me.* Rick calmed again to his logical thinking mode, a much safer mode underwater, in a narrow cave.

Rick's beam of light was reflecting off something in the center blackness. As he got closer, the panic started again. All that was reflecting at him was limestone. It appeared that the tunnel had just stopped at a dead end. Even though the water in the cave was cold, Rick's body felt a wave of heat passing over it. It was not from an underground thermal spring but a heatwave of pure fear. A heatwave of pure panic. Many thoughts rush through him. *It was probably good that Ted was not seeing this,* Rick thought. *If the cave ends here, we are screwed. There is no way we can back out now. Is this where my love affair is going to end with Mary, a dead end? Where in the hell did that thought come from?* He thought almost out loud, *"calm down." There is still a current coming from somewhere.* Rick's logical mind took over once more. He was now back in survival mode. Swimming to within three feet of the dead-end, he saw that the tunnel did not end but made a ninety-degree turn to the right. He knew they had no choice but to keep going forward, so Rick tried to make the turn. It was just too narrow. He backed up slightly and felt his swim fins hitting Ted's head. *There's no way to make that corner without removing our tanks, but that is not an option in the narrow space.* Rick tried the corner again. This time he turned completely on his side so that his stomach arced around the inside bend. His tank scraped against the backside of the wall with a muffled scraping sound. With a cloud of stirred-up silt and the eerie scrapping of limestone on metal, he was able to wiggle through the corner. Ted was watching all of this in puzzlement and fear. Fortunately, he could still see enough through the stirred-up silt to see what Rick was doing, and could follow what he did, exactly. Three feet after the bend, Rick's head poked out into a very welcomed sight. A vast cavern. He quickly swam to the far wall so that Ted had enough room to get out of the tunnel. He looked back and saw Ted wiggling through the small hole like the opening was giving birth. He was followed by his safety line that was his umbilical cord. The cavern was at least twenty feet from side to side and another twenty feet to the ceiling. It was the most beautiful cavern he had ever seen. It was so nice to swim again in open water and not be crawling. Rick kicked out into the middle of the room to meet Ted. His eyes were very large and round with fear behind his facemask. Rick was thinking he must have looked the same. Surrounded by a thick cloud of silt that he had brought out of the womb with him, he gave Rick a quick thumbs up. He straightened himself up in the open water and swam over to where Rick was floating. Rick watched Ted as he looked around the cavern and saw him feel the relief that Rick had just felt. Ted looked down at the cavern's floor and quickly looked over at Rick while pointing a finger towards the bottom. There was no floor. They both shone their beams of light down below them. They saw nothing. Their beams of light just seemed to fade away into the darkness without reflecting anything back. It was a deep hole. With the water as clear as it was, their beams of light should easily travel thirty feet. Under different circumstances, this would have been a great place to explore, just to see what was at the bottom and how far it went down. The awe of the place was quickly broken when Rick saw Ted look at his watch and motioned Rick that their air supplies were probably getting on the low side. Rick motioned back with an OK-sign and pointed to the tunnel opening. Ted gave a thumbs up of agreement. They both felt the dread of having to negotiate the corner and go back through the narrow passageway again. All the same fears and anxieties were still there, waiting for them on the return trip. At least they knew what to expect now, and they were on the way out. As they start swimming towards the opening, Ted grabbed Rick's arm and pulled out one of his flares. He made an amplified point with his index finger down into the bottom of the cavern. Rick knew right away what he was thinking. Ted lit the flare, which immediately illuminated the beauty of the underwater room. He held it up in the water for a few seconds so they could fully take in the magic of the place. Then he dropped the flare, letting it slowly float into the abyss. The falling beacon lit the sides of the shaft as it fell. It kept getting smaller and dimmer until it disappeared. *This is one deep ass, hole*, Rick thought. He knew Ted was thinking the same. Rick was still holding onto the feeling that this was an amazing place, even after all the fear and uncertainty they had just endured getting there. After a few seconds of just staring down at the nothingness, Rick tapped Ted on the shoulder and motioned for him to go ahead into the tunnel. Ted put up his hand like a traffic cop and moved it towards the opening with a long sweeping motion. Showing Rick that he wanted him to lead the way again. Rick managed to squeeze around the ninety-degree bend again, this time with a much easier movement. He halted briefly to wait for Ted. He could not see Ted behind him, but when he got the feeling that he was there, he started following their safety lines down the narrow passageway. Pulling his way along the safety lines, Rick thought, *I can't believe that some divers still don't use safety lines in these places.*

The time it took them to travel up the narrow tunnel seemed an instant compared to the time it took them to get down. It seemed like no time at all before Rick broke through into the big blue room. The light coming through the central chimney they had rock climbed down was a welcome sight. The climb up through the chimney required no effort. The strong current was now their friend and shot them out at high speed into the open pond. The beautiful green glow of the sunlight beaming down through the pond of Jell-O was a wonderful sight. Ted caught up with Rick in the open water, and as he saw the rays of sun coming through the breaks in the vegetation, he raised both of his arms like a religious pilgrim. They both just stayed motionless for a few minutes, floating under the water. They looked at each other, then spent the rest of the time appreciating the beauty of it all. They were both thinking how great life was and that just a short time ago, they were at a point where this beauty could have been lost to them forever.

Rick and Ted surfaced in the middle of the blue eye and immediately pushed their masks back onto their foreheads. While treading water, they both removed their mouthpieces at the same time. The breaths of fresh air on the surface were always a pleasant taste after a long dive, but today the air seemed so much sweeter. They just looked at each other and at the same time just said a loud, "fuck." Without saying another word, they swam as far as possible into the green slime and again started the slow walk towards the shore. There was not much conversation between them as the reality of what had just happened was fully sinking in. They were both thinking what a stupid and dangerous situation they had just put themselves through. And, of course, how lucky they were.

Mary was on the shore pulling in the safety lines as they walked in.

"It is about time you guys got here," she shouted, "We didn't time you, but we figured you had to be almost out of air."

"Oh, we had a lot of air-time left," Rick said, "We just got bored, so we decided to come in."

Ted laughed nervously.

As Rick took his first step onto the sandy beach, Mary was right there wrapping her sun-warmed arms around his cold neck.

"Did you miss me?" was all she said as she gave him a big kiss.

Mary helped Rick get off his equipment and wet suit as Sandy did the same for Ted.

"How about we go get you some lunch and a cold beer?" Mary said as she set down the heavy tank in the sand.

"Sounds wonderful," answered Rick.

Mary went to get lunch while Sandy organized the dive equipment.

Dressed in just bathing suits and a towel around their necks, Rick and Ted just collapsed on a blanket in the warm sun. They both stayed very silent until Rick finally asked Ted, "Were you as concerned about things down there as I was?"

Rick's small comment opened the valve on Ted's mouth.

"Concerned, you have got to be kidding me, right? I was scared shitless. It seemed like I was swimming into a cloud of silt at one point, and when I came out, I was in that narrow tunnel. I knew right away there was nowhere to go but forward. I can only imagine what you were thinking when you saw that ninety-degree turn."

"I didn't know it was a ninety-degree turn. I thought it was a dead end."

"Jesus' fuck," Ted said with a concerned look on his face, "I am so glad it was you in the front and not me. Ignorance is sort of nice in those situations."

"That deep hole in the cavern," Rick said, changing the subject before Mary could hear what they were talking about. "That must have been at least sixty feet deep. I can only imagine what the hell is down there."

"It would be fun to explore that," said Ted, "However, I think I might be done with cave diving. That was a little too scary and stupid for me."

"I hear you, buddy," said Rick, "I might have to give that some thought also. But it was pretty darn cool when we weren't thinking about dying, wasn't it?"

"Yes, it was."

"Are we even for my rock-climbing fear now?" Rick asked.

"Even?" Ted replied. "I don't think so. I will have to spend the rest of my life thinking how to get even with you on this one." He then slugged Rick on the arm and added, "We did make it out of there and I thank you for guiding, buddy, I don't know if I could have."

"No problem, my friend."

They leaned into each other and did a healthy man-hug.

At that moment, Sandy came running over, holding a pressure gauge in her hand. She calmly said with a hidden excitement, "A, I just put the pressure gauge on your tanks for the heck of it. Rick, you had 200 psi left, and Ted, you had 150 psi left. You two were about out of air."

"That settles it for sure," Ted said, "I am sticking to open water dives from now on."

"I might be with you on that one, buddy."

"And furthermore...."

Rick cut off Ted's conversation short, as he realized he needed to talk with Mary, who was over on the blanket, with his lunch and beer.

"Excuse me, Ted, I need to go have a talk with Mary. We can finish venting our dive later, OK?"

"No problem, buddy.

Rick walked over to Mary and sat down beside her.

"How are you doing, sweetie?" Rick asked as he gave her a kiss on the cheek.

"How are you doing is probably a better question to ask," she said with a look of concern. "It sounds like it might not have been that enjoyable a dive."

"It had its moments where I was not sure how things were going to end up."

"I was worried, you know."

There was a long silence where neither one of them could think of something fitting to say. Rick was silent, as he was trying to think of how he was going to express what needed to be said. Mary knew Rick well enough now that she sensed the rare seriousness that was radiating from him. Mary respected the silence. She also braced herself for the coming words she knew would be something she did not want to hear. She just looked at Rick with her loving eyes that had the early beginnings of tears.

"I thought about you a lot down there, you know." Rick began, "Even when things were not going well, and I should have been concentrating on breathing."

"Is that a good thing?" Mary asked.

"I think it is," Rick slowly answered, followed by another long pause. "I think that I learned a lot about myself today. I think I learned a lot about us today. I think I learned a lot about life in general. I think I learned about relationships."

"Wow, that must not have been an enjoyable dive at all," Mary said, trying to inject a little humor.

Another thirty seconds of a long silence took place.

"Are you going to share this great insight with me or is it something that I might not want to hear."

"Love is an underwater cave," Rick answered back.

"This is going to be very deep, isn't it?" Mary said regretfully, trying at humor again. Not for humor's sake but because she was scared and nervous, "I am sorry, go on," she said nervously and moved closer to Rick. The tears were now starting to flow in her eyes.

Rick grabbed her hand and looked into her eyes as he continued.

"Well, when Ted and I started down into the cave we had a lot of room to move around. The pond was large, and that first cavern was large. There was no sense of being trapped. It was just fun exploring the new territory."

"I think I see where you are going with this dear," interrupted Mary. "You're going to tie all of this to our relationship, aren't you"?

"Sort of, I guess. Don't you think that this is how love affairs start out?"

Not really wanting an answer till he finished, Rick continued, "Don't relationships always start out very wide open with all channels of possibilities to explore. Isn't the excitement extreme, and all thoughts are focused on each other. There is no room or time for anything else but each other."

"Yes, I agree," answered Mary, "and isn't that the wonderful part of it?"

"Yes, it is dear, but it always seems to change. Things get complicated. Each person has their own goals and dreams that they ignore early in the relationship. These goals and dreams eventually re-surface. The dilemma starts as to what to do next. Is the relationship worth modifying these dreams and goals? Is it worth going forward in the relationship, not knowing where things will end?

"Are you saying this is how our love affair is going?" Mary asked with a quiver in her voice.

"I think you know that it is, don't you," answered Rick

A long silence surfaced again. Then Rick continued.

"The cave changed me today. I left the open-spaced cavern and ended up in a narrow tunnel, leading to an unknown end. There was not only an unknown end, but the tunnel itself became narrower. I had the feeling of being trapped. Claustrophobia set in. I was worried about breathing, about escaping, about being able to continue to live. I had visions of suffocating and never getting out."

"You are still talking about us, aren't you?" Mary asked, with not just a quivering voice, but with tears now starting to flow down her cheeks.

"There is more to it than that," Rick answered back, squeezing Mary's hand a little tighter.

"The more the tunnel narrowed, the more trapped I felt. I could have tried to turn back, but that would have been very difficult. So, I kept going forward. When the dead-end appeared, I thought that it was the end. Things were over. I had no choice now but to end the forward movement and quit. It was too late as I could not turn back. I kept going forward. Even though it was difficult, and it was a dead end. I kept going forward until I finally broke through to one of the most beautiful caverns I had ever seen. Maybe a cavern that you might see only once in a lifetime. One that you might never see again. A cavern that saved my life. I would never have seen it if I had not kept going forward when it felt like I should have turned back. I might not even have survived if I had not kept going."

After a long silence, Rick asked Mary, "Does that make sense to you?"

"I think so," Mary answered with a questioned look on her face. "What does it all mean about us?"

"I think it means that you cannot turn back from love. You must keep going forward in a relationship like ours. A relationship that we both know is so right. No matter how trapped we feel, how difficult things get, no matter what things might try and interfere with us. With our love affair, I think we have found our big, beautiful cavern."

Mary just smiled. The tears were still in her eyes, but they were now not tears of sadness but had changed to tears of joy. Tears of love. Mary knew what Rick was trying to tell her. She put her arms around Rick's neck, and they shared a long, passionate kiss. At that moment, they experienced the most loving kiss that either one of them had ever known. A kiss that they would never forget. Rick realized that Mary knew what he was trying to tell her.

There was a long silence again as Rick had said everything he needed to say.

For a few very long minutes, they just held on to each other. They held on to each other tighter than they ever had. The warmth and the love flowed between them more than it ever had flowed before.

Rick finally broke the silence. He gently turned Mary towards him and, while looking into her beautiful brown eyes, said softly,

"You know, I have a feeling that Chicago is going to be another wonderful adventure for us.

Richard Schalhamer was a high school physics teacher before becoming a full-time writer. He has been recognized with many honors at both the local and national level, including "Teacher of the Year" for both. He retired from teaching after 25 years to fulfill a lifelong dream to become a writer. He lives on his ranch in the mountains of Colorado.

He has kept a journal since high school so much of his writing is based on real life events and real people from these well-documented accounts. Although not an officially-published writer; over the years, he has written many classroom physics stories, textbooks, and songs.

His main love is crafting romance/adventure stories, but he has also written many children's books for his two boys.

He has lived more fully than most and has embarked on countless adventures, therefore acquiring a wealth of knowledge and memories to access for inspiration.

In the past he has written for friends and students but has decided to share his writings and thoughts with the rest of the world.

Made in the USA
Middletown, DE
30 December 2021

57170513R00137